Trail of the Forgotten Grizzly

An Arizona White Mountain Adventure

Daniel Scott Deublein

ISBN: 979-8-218-29214-0

Acknowledgment

I would like to express my deepest gratitude to the following individuals whose invaluable contributions made the creation of this book possible:

To my beautiful wife, whose unwavering support and boundless encouragement were instrumental in embarking on this literary adventure. Your belief in me and your constant reminder to be as brave as the characters I was creating pushed me to surpass my limits.

To Paly Palestrant, I am forever grateful for that unforgettable New Year's Eve night when you instilled in me the unfaltering belief, not only in the attainability of writing a novel but also in my own ability to bring such a story to life.

A special mention to Joan Sullivan Garrett, whose own remarkable accomplishment in completing her book *One Life Lost, Millions Gained* served as a constant inspiration. Your resilience and dedication inspired me to persevere through challenges and reach new heights.

Jessica Roberts, collaborator, and contributor, I am profoundly grateful for your expertise, guidance, and constructive feedback. Your keen eye for storytelling, invaluable insights, and steady support elevated the quality of this book and helped shape it into its final form.

To all those who provided feedback, shared their insights, and offered encouragement along the way, thank you for being a part of this journey. Your support and belief in this project were invaluable.

Lastly, I would like to extend my gratitude to my readers, who give life to these pages. It is your curiosity, enthusiasm, and appreciation for nature that make the hours of writing and editing worthwhile. Thank you for joining me in this literary endeavor.

With heartfelt appreciation,

Daniel Scott Deublein

Contents

About the Author

Daniel Scott Deublein, a native of Show Low, Arizona, and former actor who portrayed characters such as Ben Swift on Beverly Hills, 90210, embarked on a journey that has led to new horizons. Departing from the entertainment industry in 2005, he set his sights on pursuing a Master of Science Degree from Des Moines University. Afterward, he became a board-certified Physician Associate and began practicing Emergency Medicine and Interventional Radiology. He would later go on to work in the villages of Kodiak Island, Alaska.

In a serendipitous turn, he and his wife eventually retired to the tranquil embrace of Greer, Arizona, where they built their own log home. Daniel later returned to filmmaking, crafting the compelling short film "Rooted in Arizona." It premiered at the Chandler Film Festival and received recognition as the 'Best Documentary Short 'at the Independent Shorts Awards in Los Angeles, CA.

Evolving as an author, Daniel's inaugural novel, "Trail of the Forgotten Grizzly," emerged in 2023. With a deep-rooted commitment to conservation, he actively champions the preservation of the Arizona White Mountains.

Preface

Dear Readers,

Welcome to this literary journey, and thank you from the bottom of my heart for choosing to embark on it with me. I am filled with gratitude for your interest in my book and for the time you've dedicated to exploring the pages that follow. I also want to extend my appreciation to all those who call the Arizona White Mountains their home and dutifully serve as their guardians.

As a child growing up in Show Low, Arizona, I had my fair share of thrilling experiences in the great outdoors. One particular night, while camping along the Black River with my fellow Boy Scouts, we gathered around a crackling campfire. It was then that a tale about grizzly bears roaming the White Mountains unfolded in the pitch-dark night. I can still remember how I trembled in my hiking boots, and that story stayed with me, knowing that it was not mere fiction but a true account. The fascination of grizzly bears roaming these very mountains became etched in my mind, though I soon realized that they would forever remain a distant reality.

In the process of writing this book, I delved deeper into the repercussions of species extinction. The impact on the ecological system is profound and often underestimated, affecting us in ways we are yet to comprehend fully. While conflicts between humankind and wildlife are inevitable, it is essential to seek solutions that foster mutual support and coexistence rather than wiping out entire species from our planet.

The joy I experienced while crafting this book was akin to a rollercoaster ride of emotions. As I introduce the characters to you, I reveled in placing them amidst the very areas on the mountain that have held my heart since my youth. The White Mountains of Arizona are undeniably special, and it is incumbent upon each one of us to treat them with utmost care. Whether you camp in a tent, hike for a day, or park your RV for an extended period, this land is ours to cherish and protect.

I must confess that I am neither an expert nor even an amateur in understanding the intricacies of conservation, wildlife, or ranching. I do not claim to possess all the answers, and while you may find aspects to disagree with in this book, please remember that it is simply a story I wished to share. I harbor no intention of advocating one viewpoint over another. The characters that came to life on these pages sometimes clashed with my own ideas, creating a journey of discovery that surprised even me.

In closing, I extend my heartfelt thanks to each one of you for taking the time to read this tale. May we all strive to coexist harmoniously with nature, wildlife, and, most importantly, with each other.

Happy reading, and let us cherish the boundless wonders that our world has to offer.

Warm regards,

Daniel Scott Deublein

I: Introduction

WITH AN ORANGE HUE, the sun shone brilliantly, casting a golden light across the mountain peaks. Jonathan trudged uphill and took in a deep breath of fresh air. He had hiked across the aspen glens that boasted stunning views of the mountain's foothills and was now making his way across a mixed coniferous forest that included Douglas Fir, Ponderosa Pine, and Blue Spruce. He loved everything about this: the quiet, the calm, and the breathtaking views that never failed to enthrall him even after twenty-five years as a game warden.

Jonathan had dedicated his life to nature: as a conservation officer, he'd worked mostly on preserving biodiversity in its natural form. Back then, his mission was to protect the wildlife species in Arizona, specifically the Apache-Sitgreaves National Forest, and ensure their preservation for future generations. He wished for others to come to this place and experience the same delight that he felt every day, even if they visited five, eighty, or even a hundred years from now. Jonathan used to share this with his wife, Marianne, but she passed away last year, and he had been living alone since.

They had no children, and that worked out well because the entirety of Jonathan's existence revolved around his work in forestry and its conservation. He'd been a bit lonely since Marianne passed and his friends from Phoenix asked him to move back, but Jonathan hated the pollution, hustle, bustle, and clutter of living a suburban life. He'd much rather spend his remaining years, however many there were left, enjoying the quiet tranquility of this bit of heaven on earth. The retirement stipend was comfortable, and he'd spent enough time giving to the world. Now, it was time to rest and relax.

He readjusted his cap and sunglasses as he made his way up the stunning trail. He had experimented with other routes before, but this particular one held a special place in his heart because it was Marianne's favorite. Being here felt like she was with him. He'd built his day into a routine: every day, he was awake at dawn to hear the first chirps of birds, witness the first scurrying of wild animals emerging from their homes to forage and feel the first rays of sun on his face.

After his morning round outside, he would return to his log cabin along the river and prepare a simple breakfast consisting of either oatmeal, eggs, bacon, or just black coffee. Then, he'd catch up on the local news and settle down to write. He was recording a memoir of his life. It focused mainly on his work as a game warden and the challenges that he'd encountered while trying to secure government funding for the preservation of the Arizona White Mountains. The book also touched upon the significance of the environment and how, with the advent of global warming and population growth, systems and people alike needed to take greater action to support environmental efforts. He hoped that it would help people. He had lived a complete and purposeful life; this was the legacy that he would leave behind.

In the afternoon, Jonathan would cook himself a meal on an open fire. It was typically fish these days; he'd found himself more and more gravitated towards a stream that flowed beyond his daily trail and had started fishing there regularly. Later in the day, he'd go for a long hike and return at sunset.

Once home, he'd cook himself a light dinner – usually vegetables – and then settle in by the fire with a book. Jonathan was tall and well-built with handsome, rugged features. These days, however, he needed a shave. Jonathan liked to think that he was growing a beard but was, in fact, not really bothered by trying to maintain a good appearance. He only really saw people during his evening hikes – typically couples or traveler groups – or else on his weekend shopping trips to Springerville, which he conducted every Saturday morning by driving out of the tiny mountain village of Greer.

Jonathan strolled by his stationary 1972 Land Cruiser, proceeding to ascend the wooden stairs that guided him to his log cabin. As he reached the wooden deck, he effortlessly kicked off his boots. Using only muscle memory, he slipped his feet into a pair of slippers that were conveniently placed near the front door.

After a brief dinner, he settled into the large leather armchair by the fire and opened the copy of 'On the Road to Nowhere' by Karen M. Applewhite that he'd grabbed at the library the previous weekend. It was a perfect end to his day; he could ask for nothing more.

Had he left a bookmark in this book? No, he'd just started reading it. From the heart of the book, he pulled out a folded newspaper page from the White Mountain Independent, assuming that Carley Jenkins, the new librarian had left it there by mistake. There was a map of the Apache-Sitgreaves National Forest. After he flipped the page, he saw photos of Mount Baldy's beautiful scenery, accompanied by articles about the wildlife in the region and its neighboring areas, Bear Wallow and Escudilla.

It was then that Jonathan noticed a particular article. He chuckled when he saw the headline.

"Grizzly Bear Slaughters Cow?" it read.

"They're extinct," he said to himself. Nonetheless, he started to read:

Grizzly Bear Slaughters Cow?

By Matthew Kenny, Staff Writer

Are Mexican grizzly bears really extinct? Wildlife experts claim that the last grizzly bear in Arizona was killed in 1932 and that Mexican grizzly bears have been tragically wiped off of the face of the earth since 1964. William Herder, however, begs to differ. William, otherwise known as Billy, is a cattle rancher in the Escudilla Wilderness of the Apache–Sitgreaves National Forest. On Tuesday, April 8th, Herder emerged from his home to find that one of his cows had been slaughtered. "Marigold was moo-ing well into the night. She is in heat, and neither my wife nor I thought much of it," Herder told a reporter when asked about the event. He claims that the cow was attacked by a Mexican grizzly bear. Regarding reasons to supplement his claim, Herder says, "I saw it! The moo-ing grew louder and more horrific than usual so I got out of bed and stepped outside. When I switched the patio light on, I saw the beast attacking her. I went inside to fetch my rifle and when I returned, it had vanished. Poor Marigold just lay there horribly injured. She was thrashing her head wildly against the fence. I couldn't even call the vet. I knew it was too late. There was blood everywhere. So, I put her out of her misery."

Regarding information about the extinction of Mexican grizzlies, Herder says, "Well, I know they aren't extinct anymore because I saw it with my own eyes. It was silver, and no bear looks like that!" Regarding whether he was upset about losing Marigold, Mr. Herder said, "It's nature's way. I don't interfere." On why he fetched his rifle if he didn't intend to kill the bear, Mr. Herder only said, "To scare it off."

This unforeseen incident has raised speculation about the existence of the previously thought-to-be-extinct mammal among wildlife conservation groups. The source, William Herder, is the current owner of the Dead Broke Ranch, which has been owned by the Herder family for 105 years after it was acquired from the Wiltbank family in 1917. Mr. Herder is sixty-seven years old and suffers from mild dementia following his completion of chemoradiation for hepatocellular carcinoma.

About the author: Matthew Kenny is an investigative journalist who recently graduated from Arizona State University. He is currently a staff writer for the White Mountain Independent.

Jonathan looked up and smiled. It was entirely likely that the man's cancer treatment had caused mild delusions as a side effect, but he would also like to entertain the possibility that the Mexican grizzly still existed. They were beautiful creatures, but he'd never hoped to come across one in his career because, as the article mentioned, they'd been extinct since 1964. He put the newspaper page aside, shaking his head.

Next, he stood up and went to the fridge, where he took out a cold can of beer. After getting a clean glass from the dishwasher, he brought them back to the living room and put the glass on a coffee table coaster. Using his teeth, he opened the can and settled into his armchair. He poured half of the can into the glass and then chugged the remaining, a little quirk he'd picked up recently. He tossed the can into the waste bin in the corner without leaving his chair.

Jonathan sighed as he turned his attention once again to the book that he'd been meaning to read. The fire crackled comfortably beside him. He thought he would read a couple of pages and then turn in for the evening.

Knock, knock.

Who could that possibly be? Jonathan chuckled privately to himself. He imagined how funny it would be to find a Mexican grizzly bear on its hind legs pretending to be a tourist from Phoenix. He would welcome him in, pour him a beer and then explain why he should stay in the city.

Knock, knock, knock, the door went again.

Patience, thought Jonathan as he got up.

"Coming!" he called out and walked to the door.

"Chief Grey Cloud!" he exclaimed, breaking into a smile when he opened the door.

The man standing outside was wheat-skinned and had long black hair that parted down the middle and was tied into two loose pigtails. He wore them over his shoulders, which donned an off-white fabric with gold hems that were buttoned at the forearms. He was wearing traditional knee-high leather moccasins.

The man had piercing black eyes, a strong jawline, and an equally commanding demeanor. Towards his friend, however, his eyes were softened, but his expression remained willfully grave.

"Come inside, please," said Jonathan, making way through the doorframe and taking a step back.

"I can't stay long," replied the Chief in a deep and rich voice. "Jonathan, my people and I need your help."

A slight sweat broke out at the back of Jonathan's neck as he registered the concern on his friend's face.

"What's wrong, Chief?" he asked, creasing his brow.

"The Gods have sent me here," the Chief replied ominously, looking straight ahead.

Then, he turned his gaze towards a perplexed and increasingly alarmed Jonathan and said, "In 1932, the last of the Mexican grizzly bear was killed upon our land. We both know that the US government funded and organized their extinction. My grandmother told us stories since we were children of how most grizzly bears were shot, but one survived and hid on the peak of Mount Baldy. For years, the white man tried to find it but was unable to track it down. Legend claims that it still lives, surviving on whatever means of sustenance that it can find for itself while hiding in these White Mountains. Eventually, the white man gave up his hunt, and the bear's trail was forgotten. I always weighed the possibility of its existence but assumed it was now a holy wind. That is until yesterday when I saw the bear with my own eyes. Initially, I was unsure if my eyes were playing tricks on me, but I saw it unmistakably move across the West Fork of the Black River during sunrise."

"I debated coming to you for help, but I have no choice but to seek your aid. Please help me locate the bear, and through Apache ritual, we can release this spirit. It is not alive, Jonathan, but only a trapped spirit here to reclaim the land. So speak the ancient legends of my people."

Jonathan listened intently. He hated that his friend was pleading with him.

"Chief, please come inside," he said, not looking directly at him and gesturing to the living room.

The Chief walked inside. Jonathan closed the door behind him.

"Have a seat," he said, gesturing towards the brown leather sofa by the old television set in the corner. "Would you like a beer?"

The Chief shook his head and slowly sat down on the sofa. Jonathan dragged a wooden chair from the kitchen table. He sat down on it backward, leaning his chin against the backrest.

"Chief, you know how much respect I have for you and your people, but I don't think going after this thing is a good idea. If the bear is out there, as you've seen, it's better to leave it be and not draw attention toward it. The hunters, conservationist groups, and the media will swarm this place. Plus, I'm retired."

"Such a kind woman she was," said the Chief looking over at a picture of Marianne that sat on the shelf. Jonathan turned his head around. It was from a fishing trip that they took together back when he was still a game warden. He was in uniform; she was wearing a deep blue day dress. Marianne smiled brilliantly; he smiled because of her.

Chief Grey Cloud turned towards Jonathan. "Jonathan, you are the only white man we trust. Ever since you secured and returned the satchel of Geronimo, my people have been indebted to you. Today, I am once again asking for your help –"

"Chief, please don't –" began Jonathan, but the Chief cut him off. He turned towards the shelf again.

"Your rival is already on the hunt. He will use that bear for fame."

Jonathan straightened up a bit. The Chief was referring to Dwayne Tompkins, a wily young critter from Alpine who enjoyed poaching wildlife. Jonathan had frequently tried to catch him in the act, but was unsuccessful. And ever since Marianne passed away, he hadn't given this boy much thought.

However, learning that Tompkins was on the hunt for the possible remaining member of an extinct species, Jonathan felt a surge of blood flow throughout his veins. If the Mexican grizzly was indeed alive, it should be protected and not killed.

He turned towards the Chief, who was now looking at him and locked his gaze directly.

"Where do we begin?"

II: The Journey Begins

JONATHAN PICKED UP the receiver of his landline phone and heard the hypnotic melody of the dial tone. His phonebook was open in front of him, lying on an old table beside an empty glass of water. Unlike most people, Jonathan didn't own or carry a cell phone. In fact, he advocated against the installation of cell towers in the area due to their negative impact on wildlife. Recent studies had shown that the electromagnetic radiation from these towers affected bird populations' reproduction and nesting behaviors.

There was a click as the line connected.

"Hello," said the man on the other end.

"Wagner," said Jonathan warmly, "How are you doing?"

"Mr. Crow!" said Wagner in recognition, "Yeah, I'm great! How are you?"

"Good, thanks for asking. How is work going?"

Ethan Wagner, a new game warden, had requested guidance from Jonathan a few times when he was transferred from San Parian to Apache-Sitgreaves National Forest. Jonathan smiled as he thought of how Marianne, true to her character, had invited Ethan over for dinner a few times. Unfortunately, her health took a turn for the worse, and she had to be hospitalized. Ethan would visit them both during her stay in the hospital.

"Work is great, thank you for asking! Just wrapped up another SAR."

A search-and-rescue mission was exactly the kind of thing that Ethan could do most efficiently, thought Jonathan. He was still a young man in his early thirties, but Jonathan had found him to be both reliable and responsible. And that is why he was calling him now.

"Excellent," said Jonathan, "Listen, any chance you'll be in Greer later?"

"Actually, yes. I need to post some flyers. Trying to keep these off-road vehicles on designated roads," exclaimed Ethan.

"I can't stand those things. Just chainsaws on wheels, tearing up the forest," Jonathan said, shaking his head. "Hey, how about dinner at Molly's? Does five o'clock work?"

Molly Butler Lodge was Arizona's longest continuous running guest lodge and restaurant located about forty minutes from Ethan's office, but Jonathan was scrupulous about not taking personal meetings to people's workplaces. He'd rather treat Ethan to a delicious prime rib dinner.

Jonathan looked at his watch after Ethan said, "Perfect," and then hung up the phone. Upon getting dressed earlier this morning, he had placed his grandfather's leather field watch around his left wrist. As a retirement gift, Brian Rossi had presented him with an Apple watch, but Jonathan refused to wear it. He treasured heritage, a trait that heavily influenced his work in conservation. Marianne, however, wanting to count her steps, loved the technology and wore it until her passing.

It was 8:05 a.m., which meant the library would be open. He grabbed his keys and wallet and headed into Springerville. He spent the day researching the Mexican grizzly but was surprised to find no information in the Encyclopedia Britannica. In fact, the animal was surprisingly under-researched, and Jonathan learned nothing that he didn't already know.

The species had long gestation periods resulting in females giving birth only once every three years, and the last sightings that were not confirmed happened in 1971 - seven years after they were listed as extinct. Additionally, an American Biologist named Dr. Carl B. Koford had unsuccessfully led a three-month search for the bear.

Jonathan praised the biologist for showing grit and perseverance in searching for a seemingly extinct animal for such a lengthy period of time. Although the idea of embarking on a similar mission unsettled him, Jonathan reminded himself that most people fail due to inadequate planning and give up when close to achieving success. This realization fueled his determination and restored his optimism.

At 1 p.m., he walked to a coffee shop across the street, bought himself a small sandwich, and ordered a black coffee. When he returned to the library, he flipped through a survival magazine. Much of the information that existed was to promote products and drive sales. Jonathan knew there was little utility in packing a full-scale barbecue smoker while venturing into the wild. All one needed was nutrient-dense, non-perishable food, a portable water filter, and some layered clothing.

When setting out on a backpacking trip, the tent and sleeping bag make up the majority of the weight. You can even skimp on soap because the water birch that grows along the streams contains cleansing qualities.

Jonathan, being an experienced backpacker, knew about these things that only experienced backpackers would know. He did not back away from bearing a little hardship on his travels. For him, life was not about avoiding discomfort but about learning to adjust and adapt to different situations.

He put down the magazine and reached for a map. The librarian, a thirty-year-old redhead, smiled at him briefly as he borrowed a pen.

"Thank you, Carley!" said Jonathan as he went back to the desk which he had been using. He began tracing his route but realized he needed to first understand plausible locations where the Mexican grizzly might exist.

Now that the story was out, he needed to locate the bear before the government officials, conservationists, and his rival Dwayne Tompkins did. He would need to be efficient and meticulous in his search, as it wasn't practical to cover the entire Apache-Sitgreaves National Forest. He simply couldn't waste time and resources searching the wrong areas. And, unlike Dr. Carl B. Koford, he didn't have three months.

Slightly annoyed and nonplussed, Jonathan opted to use the computer to find the information he needed. Not being technologically savvy, he approached the situation with uncertainty. He furrowed his brow as he settled in front of the darkened computer monitor, tapping a lone index finger on the keyboard repeatedly in an attempt to coax the monitor to life. Despite his efforts, the screen remained unlit, and his frustration became increasingly apparent. Just as he was considering abandoning all efforts, Carley noticed his struggle and walked over to lend a hand. Wearing a friendly smile, she reached for the power switch on the monitor and flipped it on, causing the screen to burst to life. Jonathan could not help but blush with embarrassment as he muttered a sheepish "thank you."

She let out a good-natured chuckle, "No worries, technology has its quirks. What can I help you find?"

Jonathan paused briefly as he could not disclose that he was searching for information about the Mexican grizzly bear.

"I need to Google some information," he said a little awkwardly.

She grinned, "Sure, let me show you a little trick to make your life easier."

Carley proceeded to guide him through a few keyboard shortcuts and search tips, and Jonathan's eyes widened in surprise and delight.

"Thank you!" he smiled as his confidence with the computer grew ever so slightly. As the librarian made her way back to her desk, she couldn't help but notice Jonathan's attempt to type out words using a single index finger. It made her chuckle.

The computer hummed quietly as Jonathan entered generic keywords into the search bar and clicked on every link in an effort to uncover a lead. At this point, he was beginning to wonder if it would be a good idea to contact the reporter who authored one of the articles he had found. But Jonathan chuckled to himself at the thought of having a journalist on the team. After all, he needed to move quietly because if any progress was made, a journalist would surely report it. He simply didn't trust anyone else to prioritize the bear's safety. He wished people could understand the importance of protecting wildlife, but this had been a constant battle that he had waged with the world his entire life.

He searched through numerous websites but didn't come across anything interesting or new, except for an article that talked about the Spanish conquistadors. Apparently, they had been fascinated by the Montezuma Zoo which was located in the majestic Aztec city of Tenochtitlan. The zoo housed a Mexican grizzly bear that the Spaniards had named *Oso Plateado*, meaning "silvery bear". It was the silver tip fur that made this bear unique amongst all other grizzlies.

The article dived empathically into how difficult it must have been to transport a 700-pound bear to their exotic zoo. While the article was sympathetic to the slaves who had to watch over it, Jonathan felt bad for the grizzly bear.

It also mentioned how the Aztecs exhibited the Mexican grizzly, indicating that the animal was isolated from its natural habitat, incapable of hunting or surviving in the wild and confined in unfavorable conditions. When an animal is removed from its habitat, it puts the entire ecosystem at risk.

In the modern world, the Mexican grizzly was considered a nuisance by ranchers, as they relied on cattle for their livelihood. However, killing off an animal with such a long gestation cycle radically reduced its capacity for survival.

Like people, animals instinctively choose environments where they can thrive. And keeping a single male bear inside a zoo made it impossible for it to reproduce. It was no wonder this animal was now considered extinct. Or, maybe they were just hiding.

Jonathan toyed with this idea. Grizzlies were exceptionally intelligent and had great memories. It was entirely likely that they had deliberately gone into hiding upon sensing that they were at risk of extinction due to being constantly hunted.

At 4:34 p.m., Jonathan took a drink from the water fountain at the library's entrance - he realized that as he aged, his body required more water in an effort to maintain his health. He started up his Land Cruiser, which was parked outside, and drove back to Greer to meet Ethan.

He reached Molly's at 5:02 p.m. and bumped into Ethan at the front door. They had both arrived at the same time. This is why Jonathan liked Ethan: his punctuality rendered him reliable.

"Hey!" exclaimed Ethan as he firmly gripped Jonathan's hand and shook it, "I almost didn't recognize you. Nice beard!"

Jonathan chuckled and thumped Ethan on the back. Once inside, they placed their order: John B. cut of Prime Rib, mashed potatoes with Mormon gravy, and a house salad.

"Wow," said Ethan when Jonathan told him, "A bear hunting trip. That sounds great! I'm on board. When do I pack?"

While in the hospital, Marianne had told Ethan to ensure that Jonathan didn't self-isolate when she passed away. She knew that he had a tendency to do that, and it had worried her. And judging by the state of Jonathan's appearance, he wasn't meeting a lot of people these days. Ethan privately joked to himself that the grizzly would mistake him for a brother if he showed up there – wherever there was – looking like this.

"Here's the thing," Jonathan leaned forward, "I need you to take care of the cabin. Just go there once a week.

Water the plants. Get rid of the squatters. That kind of thing."

"Once a week? How long will you be gone?" Ethan's brows were raised.

"Maybe a month, but that's a conservative estimate. I'm not even quite sure where to begin." Jonathan replied, frowning slightly.

"I'd start down on the East Fork of the Black River," said Ethan. That area, along with the Escudilla wilderness, was the primary habitat for grizzlies. In fact, off U.S. 60 at milepost 392, there sits an engraved historical marker that reads:

ESCUDILLA MOUNTAIN

DUE SOUTH RISES THE 3rd TALLEST PEAK IN AZ, REVERED BY CONSERVATIONIST, ALDO LEOPOLD ESCUDILLA WAS HOME TO IKE CLANTON OF OK CORRAL FAME & ARIZONA'S LAST GRIZZLY BEAR. IN FALL, THE NORTH SLOPE IS GOLDEN WITH ASPEN COVERING THE 23,000 ACRE FIRE OF '51. TO YOUR RIGHT, "VALLE REDONDO" NESTLES AGAINST THE MOUNTAINS

"Nah. A grizzly wouldn't be there. I mean, if it were, every camper and fly fisherman would have already seen it, right?" Jonathan leaned back in his chair, raised his arms behind him, and nestled the back of his head between his palms.

"Makes sense. We need to think like a bear."

Jonathan let out a deep, quiet chuckle.

"No, seriously!" exclaimed Ethan, "We need to think as a hunted grizzly bear would think."

Jonathan looked at him dryly, but humor glinted in his eyes.

"I think you need a wildlife biologist, someone you can trust. Maria Black, you can trust her. She would be perfect," Ethan said, chewing the last bite of his prime rib.

After graduating from Northern Arizona University, Maria Black joined Peakwest Environmental as a wildlife biologist and environmental building consultant. Following dinner, Ethan reached out to her mobile phone, sharing pertinent details about the situation, to which she responded by volunteering to meet them at the bar.

When she arrived, she immediately captured the attention of fellow bar patrons. Possessing a captivating allure, her luminous eyes held a profound depth, framed by dark-colored hair that cascaded gracefully over her shoulders. The three of them sat at a high-top table, with Jonathan ordering a beer, Maria opting for a Mojito, and Ethan being the only one who had ordered water.

"No alcohol on a weekday," he said. "It's a rule."

"You do your thing," said Jonathan, gesturing easily with his hand.

With her vivid blue eyes, Maria glanced at Ethan and then shifted her gaze to Jonathan. Then, she spoke.

'Ever since I read the Trevino & Jonkel study on the Mexican grizzly, I've always been fascinated by their findings. I'd love to get involved."

"That's exactly what I said, too!" said Ethan, raising his hand.

"Guys, this isn't a camping trip. I can handle it on my own."

"Look, Mr. Crow, I'm sure that you're more than capable of surviving alone in the mountains, but it isn't about that. We need to prioritize the bear's safety, which means that we need to get to it in time, and if this Mr. Tompkins is already on the hunt, then we need to make a move now," she said.

"Oh, you can do this alone, but my expertise in behavioral patterns of wild animals will optimize the efficiency of this mission," Maria said, "And we'd have a greater chance of success."

She put her drink down, waiting on a response.

Jonathan was impressed by her passion. It wasn't often that he met young people with such dedication toward their work. And she'd said exactly what he'd been thinking earlier. But he didn't want to admit it just yet.

"Let me be clear, this won't be a walk in the park. Passion and dedication are great, but facing an alleged extinct grizzly bear won't be easy. Should we come across it, safety will be a priority and quick sedation is crucial," Jonathan emphasized, aiming to impart some practicality to these eager young minds.

"No need to worry. I'm skilled in safely tranquilizing bears. Rest assured, we'll handle the situation with the utmost care," Maria reassured, her confident smile shining through.

Ethan's nod carried a touch of admiration.

"Impressive, Maria," he acknowledged. "I am very familiar with your skills, and you would be a tremendous asset to this mission." His words were encouraging as he looked toward Jonathan.

"Well, that's good to know, Miss Black," Jonathan said. "But we must think from all perspectives. What would be our plan of action once the bear is sedated? What is our means of transport and where will we take it? Obviously, we cannot let untrustworthy personnel get involved."

"Speaking of trust," Ethan said. "Should we be able to locate this bear, we have the support of a privately funded sanctuary. Now, this is no ordinary conservationist group; they are actually supported by an unknown, influential group operating under the radar. By being anonymous to the public, they are able to safeguard the sanctuary's existence and protection."

Maria raised an eyebrow, intrigued. "Unknown? That sounds mysterious. But what about the people working there? Can we trust them?"

Ethan smiled reassuringly. "Absolutely. The personnel there are highly trained professionals committed to the utmost secrecy and privacy of all the sanctuary's missions. They operate with strict confidentiality and understand the importance of keeping this sanctuary safe from any outside threats. I've spoken with Chief Grey Cloud, and it turns out he has connections to the sanctuary. Several tribal members are actively working there, and they're more than willing to assist on this mission."

"That's very impressive, Wagner," Jonathan said as he now felt more confident about the plan. Then he looked at Ethan and then at Maria.

"Are the two of you dating?" he spoke.

Ethan's eyes widened, and Maria blushed.

"What? No. Not at all!" they both said, talking over each other.

Jonathan grinned. "You should. You're a great fit."

He gazed through the bar windows, observing the meadow across the street as it slowly darkened. Along the banks of the Little Colorado River, a large group of elk could be seen. He realized it was already past his bedtime and recalled his wife's advice about stepping out of his shell in order to experience growth.

"Ms. Black, I'll call you in the morning. We'll need to plan our trip and get packed. We leave tomorrow afternoon."

Maria nodded solemnly and handed him her card. He placed it inside his shirt pocket and left.

The following day, he and Maria met outside Western Drug, a local market and sporting goods store located in Springerville. It was the first time in months that Jonathan had been in town two days within a week. It felt strange and surreal to witness the daily lives of people here outside of the weekend.

People were headed off to work, buses traveled to pick up the school kids, and there was an anxious energy that prevailed. A young couple walked past them on the pavement as Jonathan and Maria entered the store.

"We're going to need a map and these supplies," he said, handing her a list written on an old cocktail napkin.

"Headlamp, first-aid kit, hiking boots, oatmeal, nuts and raisins..." Maria read off some of the things on the list. "I already have some of these."

"Me too," said Jonathan, looking at her, "But I wanted to make sure that you had everything you needed."

"I'll have you know that I am very experienced in the backcountry!" exclaimed Maria.

Jonathan chuckled. "Great. Do you have a rucksack?"

"Yes."

"Do you know how to pack it?"

"Yep."

"Explain it to me, so I'm sure."

"Make sure it's no more than fifteen percent of my body weight. Pack the tent, sleeping bag, and fishing gear at the bottom, then clothes, non-perishable food items, and a portable stove near the top; we have mosquito repellent and a water purifier."

Jonathan was impressed.

As the sun climbed higher in the morning sky, they concocted their plan, leaving no detail to chance. Both of them had meticulously prepared, arranging their gear and provisions with a sense of purpose that fueled their excitement. The journey ahead held no promises, but it was a calling that neither of them could resist.

The moment had come – their meeting was scheduled for 3:30 p.m. at the Lazy Trout Market in Greer. Packing all their gear and supplies into the Land Cruiser, they embarked on their journey toward Thompson Trailhead. This was the area where Chief Grey Cloud had last seen the elusive bear.

As they drove along the rough, washboard dirt road, Burro Creek flowed gracefully in the same direction. They discussed their plan to search for clues along Thompson Trail as they backpacked along the West Fork of the Black River. Their adventure would eventually take them to Deadman Crossing, a name only spoken in hushed tones by the locals.

As they approached the final bend in the road, the remnants of Thompson Ranch came into view – a mere stem wall with an old stove nestled amidst its burned ruins.

Jonathan and Maria shared a charged glance, their eyes filled with excitement, fully aware that they were on the brink of embarking on the most thrilling adventure of their lives!

III: Trail of a Legend

JONATHAN AND MARIA parked near old Thompson Ranch and found Ethan already waiting for them.

"How did you get here?" asked Maria.

"I hiked," responded Ethan, glowing in the morning sun, his radiance a testament to recent exercise.

Ethan provided a quick update, mentioning that the Treadway Fire had now expanded to 8,400 acres. On a positive note, hand crews had managed to establish a containment line, reaching about 65% containment. He reassured them both, "You shouldn't encounter any problems."

"That's reassuring," Jonathan remarked. "Oh, I spotted a pesky mouse this morning at the cabin. Could you set a trap for that little bugger?" he inquired.

"Absolutely. As a matter of fact, I was going to head over there this evening to check on things," Ethan replied.

"Appreciate it," Jonathan said as he handed his keys to Ethan.

After exchanging a quick smile with Maria, Ethan made his way to the Land Cruiser, got in, and drove away.

"Very responsible chap," said Jonathan.

"He's nice," Maria smiled as she put on her rucksack.

As they hiked towards a section of the old railroad grade, the trail was flanked with conifers on both sides. There was a game trail leading down to the river that was covered with elk tracks and diverging between the trees. The sun was shining brightly, and the birds were chirping, setting the ideal tone for an exciting adventure.

"West Fork of the Black River is on your left," said Jonathan. "We should reach Deadman Crossing..." he glanced at his leather wristwatch, "in 35 minutes."

Maria nodded and adjusted her bucket hat. Her hair was tied into a ponytail that cascaded down her back but was, at the moment, covered by her green rucksack.

"You might want to drag that," said Jonathan, eyeing her large duffel bag.

"Oh, this?" said Maria. She was already fully engrossed in the beauty of the area.

"It's usually a good idea to conserve energy when you're on a hike."

"Won't it get dirty?" said Maria, giggling. "After all, I'm the one having to carry the dart gun and tranquilizers!"

"Lesson number one," said Jonathan, "Never be afraid of getting things dirty. You're on a hiking trip that will likely last a few weeks. You need to prioritize. A clean backpack isn't a priority at this point. Saving your energy is."

He grabbed her duffel bag and slung it onto his right shoulder.

"What about your energy?" Maria asked.

"I've done this my whole life. Carrying this amount of weight is manageable for me," he replied.

They continued to chat while hiking until the grade started going uphill. As they climbed, the river seemed to darken as the conifers thinned out.

"Oh, so that's why it's called the Black River!" Maria exclaimed.

Jonathan gave her a bemused look. "You've never been here before?" he asked.

Maria smiled sheepishly. "Only when I was kid, but I don't really remember it much."

Jonathan explained that the river appears to darken due to the tannins that get released from decaying vegetation, hence why it's called the Black River. He looked towards Maria, recalling that feeling of having experienced this place for the first time.

"You like it?" he asked.

"It's beautiful!" said Maria, "I wish more people could come here and experience it."

Then, a majestic elk with impressive antlers dipped its head below the riverbank. It drank quietly from the river, causing the water to ripple slightly. Both Jonathan and Maria came to a complete halt, captivated by the scene as time stood still. Then, in an instant, the elk raised its imposing rack and quickly trotted up the mountainside, eventually vanishing amongst the trees.

"That, right there, is the reason I got into wildlife conservation," said Jonathan, "To preserve nature's original state so that more people can experience these kinds of moments."

Looking upward at the sky, he pondered, "You know, sometimes I feel like it's just me. But don't you think these moments wipe away all of life's distractions and force you to focus on what is really important?" Jonathan inquired.

Maria smiled. "I do," she said quietly. "My love of nature started when I was a kid. I used to spend my summers at my grandparents' cabin over in Hidden Meadow Ranch. The scent of the pine trees and the bugling elk was like a soothing lullaby to me."

"Sounds amazing," Jonathan responded. "What was it about those trips that made you connect with nature?"

"It was that feeling of complete freedom, the way time seemed to slow down as I explored hidden trails, fished the trout pond, and rode horses up to Carnero Lake. I remember one evening, sitting by the campfire, looking up at the stars that seemed to go on forever. It was at that moment I realized how small yet connected I was to the world around me," she responded.

They continued their ascent. Then, the two of them stopped for a drink of water. Jonathan climbed down to the bank.

"Have you ever filtered river water before?" he asked Maria, who rolled her eyes.

"I've been camping before, Jonathan!" she laughed.

She pulled out her water filter, packed neatly at the top of her rucksack, and attached it to her water bottle. She placed the tubing into the ripples and started pumping.

"Sorry. I don't mean to put you down," Jonathan said.

"It's okay, I understand," Maria said, "You have a lot of experience and haven't met a lot of people who do."

Jonathan thought that was probably his own fault. He hadn't exactly socialized much. Marianne had always been the one who pushed him to interact with new people and ever since her passing, he'd been his old withdrawn self again.

It felt good to interact with a young person. Her perspective was refreshing.

They heard a rustle from behind and quickly turned around.

"Who—" began Maria.

"Shush," mumbled Jonathan thinking it might be wildlife.

A man emerged from behind the shrubs. Jonathan tensed up when he saw him. Then, he felt rage pile up.

"Tompkins," he breathed in recognition.

Dwayne Tompkins was wearing a khaki shirt, matching pants, and a straw cowboy hat. He was a notorious criminal and was being hunted by the authorities for illegal poaching. His mouth curled up into a horrible leer that was made sinisterly comical by the gap set between his front teeth.

"Juan, my old buddy!" exclaimed Dwayne. "What you two doin' out here?"

The shrubs rustled again, and two other men appeared from within the willows. Dwayne glanced behind him and then back at Jonathan.

"Meet my crew, Levi and Cash," he said, gesturing towards the two men.

Jonathan felt his pulse quickening.

"And who's the pretty lady?" said Dwayne, cocking his neck to glance over at Maria, who was standing just a few feet behind Jonathan.

"Get out of here before I report you," Jonathan said.

Dwayne frowned, clicked his teeth and said, "That's not very friendly, is it?"

He cocked his neck further, trying to get a full view of Maria.

Maria stood there clutching her water bottle. She took a step forward but then saw that Jonathan was seething. His temple was pulsing and he had a clenched fist.

"We just out here on a grizzly hunt," Dwayne said with a menacing insouciance, "Please be a dear and don't cross our path again."

Then, he turned around and began to walk back to where he'd come from.

Jonathan was absolutely boiling with rage. If Maria hadn't been there, he would have knocked those gapped teeth out of Tompkins's mouth.

Their animosity had begun a few years ago when Tompkins had shot a bighorn sheep in Alpine. He had come to Jonathan's house the night before, requesting some lodging under the guise of being an explorer.

All of the cabins had been closed off to renters in those days in an effort to protect the area from poachers. Several cases had been reported and investigated, but officials couldn't find the responsible party. Jonathan, then already retired and enjoying the quiet life, hadn't run into anyone new for a whole month.

So, when Tompkins knocked on his door, he was slightly glad to meet someone. And when he requested lodging for the night, Jonathan obliged.

Marianne had been extremely hospitable. She loved having people over and was always encouraging Jonathan to make more friends. She had served them hot coffee and biscuits while Tompkins and Jonathan sat by the fire in their living room. They had talked for several hours, during the course of which Tompkins had become intimately familiar with Jonathan's dedicated efforts toward wildlife preservation.

And then he had gone and shot a bighorn sheep. Jonathan found out when he'd read the paper the next day. The poaching had occurred just one mile west of U.S. 191. While there was an eyewitness who identified Tompkins in the area, there was a lack of evidence to officially charge him with any crime.

Regardless, there was no forgiveness for his deception. Jonathan was angry for not having connected the dots. There had been no other travelers in the area when the poaching had been reported. Stupid.

He turned towards Maria and said, "Wait here!"

Seeing how angry Jonathan looked, Maria didn't dare defy him.

Jonathan trudged up behind Dwayne and his crew. He climbed the steep hill and then began following them. He could make out their forms in the distance, all clad in khaki clothing, black boots, and straw hats. They entered a clearing just ahead.

"Hey!" Jonathan cried, but it was more of a roar.

Dwayne's crew, which now had two more men, stopped and turned around. The poacher himself did it slowly and menacingly.

"What's up, Crow? Miss the wifey?"

"SILENCE!" Jonathan bellowed. He didn't know if Tompkins knew about Marianne, but this was a low blow if he did.

He strode up to Dwayne and gripped his collar. His shirt started curling up within his fist. His crew immediately launched themselves and grabbed Jonathan from behind.

Suddenly, the resounding thud of hooves echoed through the air, capturing their attention. Approximately fifteen Apache tribal members were on horseback, dressed in their regalia and donning leather moccasin boots. They quickly encircled Jonathan, Dwayne and the remaining men.

"Stop this fighting at once," one of them said. His long, black hair was tied into a single braid behind his back while the rest of them wore it in pigtails. Jonathan knew that was a representation of his superiority.

"This is the land of my people," he continued, "We will not allow violence here."

Jonathan let go of Dwayne's collar, and the rest of the men let go of him.

One of the Apaches dismounted his horse and walked up to Dwayne.

"Excuse me, Mr. Tompkins, do you happen to have a copy of your special use permit?" he inquired.

Dwayne began patting his pockets, pretending to search for his permit while looking at this crew.

"Why, indeed, I do have it. Golly, it seems I left it back at our camp. Our campsite is only about 8 miles from here, but we're traveling on foot, not horseback. Would you care to follow us back there?" Tompkins suggested, fully aware they would likely decline the invitation.

"Mr. Tompkins, continue with your activities. Just a reminder, you're on tribal land. Should we catch you engaging in any unauthorized hunting, you'll be arrested immediately. Have you ever experienced time in tribal custody, Mr. Tompkins?" the Apache inquired.

Tompkins remained quiet.

"I presume not, or you wouldn't be standing amongst us today," the Apache replied.

Dwayne scowled at Jonathan and then signaled his crew of men to follow him.

"Mr. Crow," the Apache man addressed with a nod, "a pleasure to find you in our midst. Chief Grey Cloud has sent us," he conveyed. "How can we be of service?"

Jonathan gestured toward the spot where Dwayne and his crew had vanished among the trees.

"We made a mistake by allowing them to leave," he voiced. "He's here to kill the grizzly!"

IV: Shadow of the Bear

"TRYING TO KILL THE GRIZZLY?" asked the Apache man.

"Yes!" exclaimed Jonathan, his eyes wide and searching the forest for a glimpse of Tompkins. Unfortunately, the trail that he'd disappeared down was now empty and motionless.

"Do not worry," said the man, striding up to Jonathan and placing a hand on his shoulder in a gesture of reassurance, "the grizzly is not alive but a spirit from another world and cannot be caught."

Jonathan shook his head.

"Where is the Chief now? We need to tell him."

His plan was to dispatch some tribal members in the direction in which Tompkins disappeared. This would hopefully restrict the poacher's movement and allow him and Maria to reach the grizzly first.

"Come," said the Apache man, "Let us go to the Chief."

"Wait," said Jonathan. He turned around and looked upstream. He took a few long strides, then broke into a casual sprint. He hadn't realized the distance he had covered nor the time it had taken to chase down Tompkins.

"Maria!" he called out.

"I'm here," she said.

She had already climbed up from the river and was dragging both of their rucksacks, one in each arm.

Jonathan rushed forward and grabbed both of the rucksacks. He slung them over each shoulder.

"What happened?" asked Maria as they switched directions and began walking towards the tribal members.

"He and his men took off. We need to figure out a way to restrict their motion." Jonathan replied, repeating his earlier thoughts aloud.

"How would we do that?" asked Maria, but then caught sight of the Apache tribesmen in the clearing, "Are they willing to help?" she inquired.

"Exactly," said Jonathan with a smile. He was pleased that this young individual was so intelligent.

The Apache leader escorted both Jonathan and Maria toward the Chief's location while the other tribesmen dispersed. They followed his horse along an uncharted path into the forest. They then approached what appeared to be an Apache camp.

The White Mountain Apache Tribe has a deep spiritual connection with nature, which coincided with Jonathan's own core beliefs. This bond, along with his prior commitment to the tribe, granted him the opportunity to visit places that other 'white men' weren't permitted.

Without hesitation, the Chief immediately dispatched several members of Apache men in every direction. They were instructed to locate Dwayne and his crew, and if found, to immediately notify tribal authorities.

"Let's go," said Chief Grey Cloud.

"Chief," Jonathan contested, "I'm not sure if you should join us on this adventure. Maybe you should rest awhile. Plus, you have plenty of responsibilities here."

After all, his health had been deteriorating in recent months.

"Jon," replied the Chief, "I will join you on this journey. The two of you are guests to my people and it would be highly inappropriate, in this consideration, to let you wander into reservation land alone. And as far as attending to my responsibilities," he said, turning towards the young man with the single braid, "My son, Bidzil, is more than capable of doing it."

With a grin on his face, Bidzil, a name representing strength, wore his authority with a sense of pride.

It was time for Jonathan, Maria and Chief Grey Cloud to head deeper into the White Mountains and locate the bear.

Before they could set out for their expedition, Chief Grey Cloud asked Maria and Jonathan to wait. As they obliged, the Chief changed into his traditional clothing. He came out wearing traditional buckskin clothing decorated with intricate beadwork and vibrant patterns. Feathers and other natural elements were also incorporated into his outfit, symbolizing the tribe's connection to the spirit world and the natural environment. The high boot moccasins had a distinctive up-turned toe, which was decorated with different beads.

He then painted a bear on one side of his face, a symbol of strength and protection. Then, on the other side, he carefully crafted an arrow, a potent emblem of war paint that signified his readiness for Dwayne Tompkins.

Jonathan and Maria eyed him with respect.

The Chief observed the curious expressions in Maria and Jonathan's eyes. "Wearing traditional attire while engaging the spirit world is customary practice," he explained. "By donning our ancestral dress, we seek the assistance of our ancestors in establishing a connection with the spirit bear."

They both nodded understandingly.

As the trio began to climb uphill, the summer day stretched endlessly, allowing the sun to continue its radiant presence. Maria's steps exhibited a determined energy, surpassing Jonathan while the Chief ascended with effortless grace.

Jonathan wasn't exactly sure how the Chief could do it. It felt, slightly as though he had total command over the forest, as if nature unfolded itself before him. There was a connection there that he could only appreciate.

Despite her background in wildlife biology, Maria had been recently distracted from the wilderness due to the demands of her job. This separation led her to recognize a palpable disconnection between civilization and the natural world. A perplexing contradiction struck her: why would people from the city embark on journeys to these pristine landscapes for camping and fishing, only to depart, leaving behind smoldering fire and litter? The incongruity simply defied logic.

After covering countless miles, not a single sign of the grizzly had crossed their path. Could it actually be some sort of spirit bear? The question lingered; did this bear even exist?

As they pressed on, the trail became increasingly challenging as the tall grass started to thicken. The sun lazily transformed into a warm shade of orange.

Amidst the dense forest, they kept venturing deep into the wilderness in search of that elusive grizzly bear. Chief Grey Cloud seemed to know his way into the forest and led the way with his vast knowledge of the land.

As they trekked through the dense forest, the Chief's steps began to falter, his breaths becoming heavier with each passing minute. Despite the clear signs of his discomfort, he tried to hide it from Maria and Jonathan, not wanting to worry them. However, Maria noticed the Chief's occasional grimaces and exchanged a worried glance with Jonathan.

"What do you think? Is he going to be okay?" she asked with a worried expression.

"I don't know. He does seem to struggle climbing these hills," Jonathan murmured.

He then called out to him, "Hey, Chief, are you okay?"

"Never better," the Chief smiled and turned quickly to lead the way.

Following him, they reached a clearing, and the Chief paused to catch his breath, pretending to take in the breathtaking scenery. His hand discreetly reached into his pocket, pulling out a handkerchief stained with dark-colored blood. Fear and concern crept into his eyes, but he quickly concealed it, folding the handkerchief away.

Sensing the Chief's uneasiness, Jonathan said, "We've searched enough for today. We should set up camp."

Maria and the Chief agreed. They unraveled their respective rucksacks and set up their tents along the confluence of the Black River. While Jonathan and Maria prepared to camp, Chief Grey Cloud walked downstream.

As the sun set, Maria started a small fire when the Chief reappeared, pulling out a large Apache trout from his pack.

"That is too kind," said Jonathan, resisting the Chief's offer to share his dinner with him.

Maria seconded him.

"Eat. The waters have gifted us this meal," said the Chief. "The Apache trout is an ancient fish who will grant us wisdom."

Historically, the Apache Trout inhabited the headwaters of the White River, which only exists in Arizona. While it faced extinction in the 1960's due to overfishing and habitat degradation, it was rescued in 1973 when placed under the Endangered Species Act.

Jonathan always thought of the Apache Trout as an iconic species, serving as a symbol of why conservation was so important. After all, you couldn't find the Apache Trout anywhere else in the world!

While ordinarily, catching and consuming an Apache trout is against current rules and regulations, it was with Chief Grey Cloud's blessing that they cleaned the fish and cooked it over an open fire.

Following dinner, Jonathan and Maria went into their respective tents for a good night's rest. However, Chief Grey Cloud wanted to take an evening stroll before retiring.

The next day, the morning sun began to cast its golden rays upon the tranquil landscape surrounding the bank of the Black River. The air, mixed with the sweet scent of pine and damp earth, urged Jonathan to emerge from his tent. Extending his arms and taking a deep breath, he scanned his surroundings, eager to witness the beauty of the dawn. His eyes fell upon Maria, who was perched on a moss-covered rock at the river's edge. A casual grin crept across his face.

Maria appeared to be lost in the beauty of the scene before her, captivated by the rhythmic flow of the Black River.

"Good morning, Maria!" Jonathan spoke as he made his way toward her.

Maria turned her attention toward Jonathan and smiled.

"Good morning, Jonathan. Isn't it fascinating how nature has a knack for embracing the soul?"

"It does, indeed," sighed Jonathan as he took a moment to absorb the splendor of his surroundings. He glanced around, suddenly noticing the absence of the Chief.

"Where's Chief? Didn't he set up his camp?"

Maria's expression wavered for a moment. "No, he didn't. When I woke up, I couldn't find him. I assumed he had already set off on a morning stroll. But he's been gone for quite some time now."

Just as their conversation turned toward the Chief's whereabouts, a rustling sound emerged from the edge of the forest.

Both Jonathan and Maria turned their heads to find the Chief making his way toward them with his measured and deliberate steps.

"Good morning, you two," he said. "I see you are already awake. I apologize for my absence. I ventured deep into the forest with the hope of establishing a connection with the spirit bear. The spirit is wise and will not appear before us today, we must continue to earn its trust."

"We were just appreciating the serenity of this place," Maria told him.

The Chief smiled understandingly.

"Shall we continue?" the Chief asked.

"Yeah, sure. How about I get some breakfast ready, then we'll leave?" Jonathan asked.

Both Maria and Chief Grey Cloud nodded.

As the trio resumed their morning activities, a magnificent osprey swooped down towards the river, its keen eyes locked onto its target - a rainbow trout surfaced as the hatch started to release. Suddenly, the osprey plucked the trout out of the stream and soared into the sky, carrying it towards a nearby perch. Its wings beat with a sense of accomplishment.

"Wow, did you see that? The osprey's precision is just incredible!" Jonathan said admiringly.

"Unbelievable!" Maria acknowledged.

"Absolutely" said Chief Grey Cloud. "Witnessing the harmony of predator and prey reminds us of the delicate balance within the world around us."

Shortly after they finished breakfast, they packed up their tents and continued their journey. At this point, they all would be content with just seeing the shadow of the bear!

Continuing their journey until noon, each step they took became more arduous as the trail grew increasingly challenging. Despite the adversity, Chief Grey Cloud led the way, guiding them along the Malapais stone trail. Thus far, the search for the Mexican grizzly bear had proven fruitless, as no signs of its presence could be found.

With the last rays of the sun casting its shadows, Jonathan suggested setting up their camp near Caldwell Cabin - an old 1920's homestead cabin that was now managed by the forest service. The other two agreed.

As they left the river bank, they ascended up a draw to the top of the canyon. Once they located a good spot, the three of them started setting up their tents.

As Johnathan started to gather some firewood, a sudden shift in the air signaled the impending arrival of storm clouds. The distant rumble of thunder echoed through the canyon below, gradually growing louder and more ominous.

"It's gonna rain," stated Maria as she scanned the sky. As soon as the words escaped her mouth, rain began to come down with a stupendous power and started hitting them like bullets, as a burst of thunder rumbled across the sky, quickly followed by a fierce bolt of lightning. Aware of the inherent danger of seeking shelter in a tent, they ran towards Caldwell Cabin.

To their dismay, the cabin had not been rented, and its doors were securely locked. They remained beneath the protective overhang of its front porch.

The rain continued to pour for more than two hours as flashes of lightning illuminated their campsite in the distance, casting eerie shadows upon the soaked ground. Setting up camp on top of the canyon in the midst of the monsoon season now seemed like a foolish decision.

Jonathan couldn't help feeling a tinge of stupidity for choosing such a dangerous location. Suddenly, a blinding bolt of lightning sliced through the stormy sky, momentarily illuminating the entire landscape. Jonathan's heart skipped a beat as he watched it strike a tall, ancient tree a few yards away from the cabin. A sound of ripping wood echoed through the air, causing the cabin deck to tremble beneath their feet.

Before they could comprehend what had happened, sparks started flying from the point where the lighting had struck, igniting the dead fuel scattered on the ground that lay next to the cabin. A large pine tree was now engulfed in flames; the boiling sap was flickering in the air, causing a small ground fire beneath the tree.

Panic engulfed Jonathan, Chief, and Maria as they realized the danger they were in.

Fueled by a surge of adrenaline, Jonathan sprang into action. He quickly grabbed a shovel that was lying next to the campfire ring; in order to save the cabin, he needed to remove the ground fuel around it. Maria and the Chief followed him, hastily using their hands to remove all of the dead brush that lay on the ground. The rain pounded on them mercilessly, drenching them to the bone as they fought against the approaching flames.

As the tree blazed with flames, Johnathan realized that it posed an imminent danger to the cabin. Without hesitation, he grabbed hold of a ladder that was leaning against the cabin wall and ascended onto the roof, fully aware of the danger he was placing himself into. He pulled the ladder up onto the roof and cautiously maneuvered his way toward the burning tree. He urged Maria and Chief Grey Cloud to seek shelter beneath the porch. In a critical moment, as the tree threatened to collapse upon the cabin, Jonathan swiftly raised the ladder and pressed it firmly against the burning trunk as he diverted its course away from the cabin. The cabin had been saved.

Luckily, Mother Nature sensed their desperation, drenching the flames entirely. As the rain quit and the storm clouds left, the area was left in disarray, marked by the charred remains of the fallen tree and the smoky aftermath of the fire.

As they walked back to check on their campsite, Maria's tent was nowhere to be found. Like a kite, it had been ripped off the stakes and was no longer visible. Chief Grey Cloud turned to Maria with a reassuring smile.

"Maria, you can use my tent," he offered generously. "I rarely use it anyway."

Maria's eyes welled up with gratitude as she nodded. "Thank you, Chief. I appreciate it more than words can express."

She felt terrible as she questioned the method by which she used to secure her tent. She gathered the rest of her belongings and went to the Chief's tent.

"You also take some rest. Tonight's adventure must have exhausted you. Nature wants to test our resilience, and today we succeeded," the Chief said to Jonathan.

He could only smile.

With a final nod, Jonathan retreated to his tent and prepared to sleep.

Jonathan awoke the next morning with the rising sun. As he unzipped his tent, he noticed that the Chief was not there. He stepped outside of his tent, catching the sight of the smoldering tree in the distance. He was befuddled. Where was the Chief?

He caught the sight of Maria standing off in the distance; her face turned towards the sunrise. She turned to Jonathan as she heard his footsteps approach.

"Would you look at that?" she spoke.

Jonathan smiled knowingly.

"Have you seen the Chief?" he asked her.

But before Maria could respond, a voice from behind them said, "Yá'át'ééh."

They turned around and caught the sight of the Chief with a wide grin on his face.

"Nature has spoken," said the Chief. "We must go."

Jonathan made a quick breakfast consisting of biscuits and coffee and then they set out. While Jonathan was curious about where the Chief was all night, he knew that it would be inappropriate to ask.

The truth is, the Apache people are deeply intertwined with the spirits of nature and their rituals could be quite unconventional at times. Out of respect, it was best not to ask.

As they hiked downstream, the canyon grew rockier as they approached Rattlesnake Point. The rocks began to turn reddish in color and grew larger as they progressed. Each step grew increasingly cautious, mindful of the expanding growth of poison ivy that densely covered the surrounding area.

"Follow me," said the Chief as he started hiking up a small stream that dumped into the river. Suddenly, a 135-foot waterfall appeared within the canyon. With all of Jonathan's experience in the White Mountains, he'd never come across this place. It was magical.

"This is Pacheta Falls," said Chief Grey Cloud. "See that cave there? It's the entrance to a spirit world. Souls of our ancestors who travel this forest must cleanse themselves in the waterfall before reentering. We will do the same."

As they climbed up the rocky terrain, which became very slick from the water and moss, they each dipped their heads into the waterfall as they approached the dark cave.

"I wonder what's in there!" exclaimed Maria as Jonathan shook his head in awe of this place.

Maria was behaving like a young child and it was a sweet sight to witness. She dislodged her rucksack from her shoulders and pulled out a glow stick. She snapped the ends together and treaded apprehensively towards the cave.

"Do not be afraid, my child," said the Chief.

Jonathan placed a headlamp on his head and turned it on. The pitch-black color of the cave gave way to the lights and unveiled its walls. Rocks tumbled underneath their feet as Jonathan, Maria, and Chief Grey Cloud treaded carefully further inside it.

They stretched out their arms and gripped the walls as they moved to maintain balance. From experience, Jonathan knew that the grounds of caves could sometimes be counterfeit, meaning that the rocks could have been placed later, either naturally or artificially, and could tumble, leading to a fall.

Jonathan's headlamp cast a yellow glow onto some patterns on the ridged wall.

"Look!" exclaimed Maria when she saw them. All three of them stopped, and Jonathan readjusted his light to cast a glow upon the wall.

"Petroglyphs and cupules ..." breathed Maria in astonished wonder.

Jonathan stretched out his hand and gently touched some of the patterns. These rock art patterns provided invaluable insights into those who created them. Among the petroglyphs were images of wildlife, spirals representing life cycles and a single handprint. However, set slightly above all of these symbols was the silhouette of a single bear.

Jonathan turned around to look at the Chief, who was standing behind them. The Chief could recognize by Jonathan's expression that he understood the true meaning of this place.

"Nature and its forces. Let's not go any further," the Chief said. He then quietly turned around and chose to leave the cave.

Both Jonathan and Maria followed, feeling somewhat transformed after their return to the world in the sun. They experienced a profound sense of witnessing something sacred, an occurrence that felt both peculiar and mysteriously prophetic.

"Come," said the Chief, beginning to climb the ridged surface of the large rocks.

Jonathan and Maria followed him. When they climbed over the large set of rocks, they saw a plateau to their right. On the left, there was a further ascent. The Chief was already making his way towards it, with Jonathan and Maria not far behind.

Intermittently coughing, the Chief seemed to grapple with regaining his breath as he hiked in silence. Suddenly, a surge of inspiration emanated from his eyes, enabling him to finally catch his breath. It was as if the petroglyphs had conveyed a message, now guiding him under the influence of a special force

His silence seemed palpable somehow; there was a focus and direction to it. And neither Jonathan nor Maria had the courage to break it. They made their way steadily up the rocky terrain, climbing, heaving themselves upwards, and then walking with purposeful strides.

Abruptly, the Chief stopped. He motioned for them to be silent. He pointed his index finger outwards. They saw what he had seen – which had caused a stunned look in their eyes: the silvery, quiet silhouette of a bear disappearing behind a cliff.

It was less than 40 yards away!

Jonathan started to hurry towards it. He flung his bag over a rocky fissure and then jumped over it. Then, he turned around and stretched out his hand toward Maria. She imitated his motion and then jumped over the fissure as well. The Chief followed as the three of them made their way to the cliff where the bear had disappeared behind the rocks.

As they reached the area where the bear had wandered, they encountered a sheer cliff, towering approximately one hundred and fifty feet in height, leading to a dead end. No trace of the bear could be found; it had simply vanished.

Both Jonathan and Maria were entirely confused.

The Chief finally broke his silence.

"Allow me to tell you a story," he said in a wistfully authoritative voice. Jonathan could sense the nostalgic tone that caused him to pause.

"There is an urban legend," began the Chief. "Many years ago, this area was in the middle of Apache land. It belonged to my people. Those petroglyphs that you saw," he said, pointing towards the direction where they'd come from, "were created by my ancestors. They left us a message. Back then, this area was believed to be possessed by evil spirits, and nobody would dare to venture close to it. But then, a man called Jack Sullivan braved his way into this wilderness. One might call him foolish or brave, or both, but he was, in fact, an immigrant who knew nothing of this place. He was a fur trader. He would hide his grizzly pelts in a cave, which he sold to make large sums of money.

"Hearing about these silvery pelts, people from Springerville started following him, but he was a clever man with an evasive personality. The funny thing is," said the Chief, his voice growing slightly softer, "those people who followed him were never found. They went missing. Their bodies undiscovered."

"One day," he continued, "it is believed that Mr. Sullivan himself slipped on a rock and plunged to his death. The location of his hidden pelts was never found. His body was never found either. Some people believe that Mr. Sullivan had struck a deal with the evil spirits: they rewarded him with wealth in return for a blood sacrifice for the Apache people who lived here."

"It was no coincidence," said the Chief. "We saw the silhouette of the silvery bear disappear without a trace in the same location that birthed the Sullivan legend – disappearances and spirits. Petroglyphs do not lie."

Jonathan climbed back up to where the Chief stood and asked, "Are you telling me we are actually chasing a ghost?"

The Chief remained silent.

V: Unveiling the Ghost

THE ROARING CASCADE of water created a symphony of sound, drowning out their whispers. A mist swirled around them, casting a veil of secrecy over the ancient rocks, imbuing a scene that felt out of this world.

Maria's eyes scanned their surroundings, her voice barely a hushed breath.

"Jonathan, this place is mesmerizing. It feels like we've stepped into a whole different realm."

Jonathan bowed his head, his gaze fixed on the glistening water. "I agree. These falls are clearly a special place for the Apache people. Certainly, a place where legends and reality seem to intertwine."

Their attention was momentarily diverted when Chief Grey Cloud pointed toward the ground. "Look, over here," he whispered, his voice filled with reverence, "bear tracks."

Jonathan's heart skipped a beat as he followed the Chief's gaze. It was, in fact, the trail of the forgotten grizzly, a remarkable discovery.

"It's actually real," he muttered to himself.

The trio approached the tracks cautiously as if approaching something sacred. Maria knelt down, studying it with a mix of scientific fascination and reverence.

"It could be a large black bear," she said as she pulled out her measuring tape, placing it near the outmost points of one print.

She meticulously jotted down the track impressions in her notebook, ensuring thorough data collection. Meanwhile, Jonathan and the Chief stood nearby, patiently awaiting her conclusions.

"This is amazing," she whispered, barely audible to anyone but herself. "Can you believe it? These tracks... they belong to a grizzly! This bear has just rewritten the history books!"

Chief Grey Cloud's eyes gleamed with a profound sense of connection. He spoke the least amongst them as if his communications were reserved for an internal dialogue with the spirits, guiding him towards the truth they sought.

Jonathan's mind raced with possibilities. "Maria, it might be a good idea to have that tranquilizer ready."

"We must not harm the bear in any way," Chief Grey Cloud interjected before she had a chance to offer.

Maria nodded, a determined look on her face. "I understand your concerns, Chief, but rest assured I am of the same philosophy as you. No harm will come to the bear. Based on my measurements of these tracks, this bear weighs about 300 kilograms, so the dosing of the tranquilizer will be very accurate; you can trust me."

Suddenly, a loud crashing sound was heard behind them, quickly followed by silence.

An eerie stillness settled over each of them, the forest holding its breath.

And then, the impossible happened.

The mighty silhouette of the Mexican grizzly materialized on the ridge above them. Its presence was both commanding and majestic.

Chief Grey Cloud's breath caught in his throat as he witnessed the embodiment of legends before him. Its massive frame was an awe-inspiring sight. Its coat, a shimmering tapestry of silver, seemed to ripple in the soft light, hinting at a hidden strength and resilience. Each strand of fur caught the delicate glow, creating an ethereal aura around the magnificent creature.

As the bear's head turned, the fading rays of the sun caught in its eyes, transforming them into pools of liquid amber. Wisdom and ancient knowledge seemed to reside within those depths, telling tales of untamed wilderness and generations past. Every movement was purposeful as it slightly lowered itself to the ground. From the tip of its broad snout, a crown of silver fur traced a path along the bear's strong jawline. The creature's ears, alert and perceptive, twitched with a heightened sense of awareness, attuned to every rustle and breath of the forest.

As the silver grizzly stood upon the ridge, the air seemed to bow to its presence. One could feel the weight of history, the echoes of a forgotten era, and the fragile balance between humanity and the untamed forces that once shaped the natural world.

Chief Grey Cloud whispered, his voice filled with awe, "The spirits of the ancients live within. I sense my ancestors are protecting it."

Jonathan's heart pounded with a mixture of exhilaration and trepidation.

"Remarkable," he said, thinking that Marianne somehow was also present for this majestic moment.

As they stood there, a profound realization washed over them; they had to act quickly before the bear disappeared into thin air, as per its elusive nature.

As Maria's finger caressed the trigger, the tension was almost palpable. With a surge of determination, she squeezed the trigger, releasing the dart that soared through the air, finding its mark in the majestic presence of the silver grizzly bear.

Jonathan's eyes widened with a mixture of relief and excitement. "Maria, you did it!"

A surge of triumph mixed with relief washed over Maria's face as she nodded. "Let's be cautious. An intramuscular injection of Ketamine for this size of the bear will take several minutes. I'm just glad we found it before the poachers!"

Chief Grey Cloud's eyes gleamed with gratitude and respect. "We have protected the spirit and allowed its sacred existence to continue for future generations."

As the bear's colossal form began to sway, its movements growing sluggish, the trio retreated to a safe distance, a shared understanding passing between them. They watched as the bear's breathing slowed and its powerful muscles gradually relaxed.

Maria's voice was filled with reverence. "Ketamine does cause transient amnesia, so the bear won't recall this experience."

The sedative worked as the bear slipped into a tranquil slumber.

"Let's go!"

With a steady hand, she skillfully placed an IV catheter into the bear's cephalic vein, securing it in place. Above, she suspended a liter of normal saline from a sturdy branch while checking its vital signs.

Jonathan nodded, his voice laced with determination.

"We cannot let Tompkins and his crew of poachers get their hands on this bear. We must stay vigilant and ensure its safety."

Chief Grey Cloud's face hardened with resolve.

In the depths of these White Mountains, a symphony of celebration seemed to resonate as if the spirit of Mother Nature rejoiced in the bear's rescue.

With the safety of the Mexican grizzly bear at the forefront of their minds, Jonathan, Maria, and Chief Grey Cloud swiftly initiated the next phase of their mission.

It was at this point that Jonathan realized that he should have kept up with the times. Of course, he'd mapped out what they were going to do once they found the bear beforehand, but he still recognized and appreciated the benefits that technology offered.

"Can you call Ethan?" Jonathan inquired of Maria.

"This far up in the mountains? There's no cell service. Luckily, I packed a sat phone," she said with a smile. "Ethan is on speed dial!"

Maria pressed the number one and handed the phone to Jonathan.

"Wagner, can you hear me?" Jonathan asked, fumbling with the abnormally large device. "Never mind how I'm calling you. Send that private helicopter to our location and remember what we discussed," he reminded Ethan about the mission's secrecy.

The only person that he could trust with this, of course, was Ethan. The mission would have to be top-secret. Already, he felt his stomach turn at the thought of what could happen if Tompkins and his crew caught a whiff of their discovery. He would see the helicopter overhead for sure if he was anywhere within a few miles of them, so they would have to be deft with their operation.

They waited; it would take at least an hour. In the meantime, they watched the bear in its slumber. They could hardly believe what they were witnessing. It seemed like a fortuitous miracle. The bear was unrealistically beautiful, and its presence almost holy.

As it breathed slowly in and out, Maria cast her eyes to the heavens and whispered a prayer of gratitude. Jonathan thought about how many more of these miracles would be witnessed and experienced by people around the world if they gave nature the reverence that it deserved.

As time passed, the rhythmic thumping of rotors filled the air. With eager anticipation, the trio observed as the helicopter gradually descended from above, gracefully touching down in a clearing adjacent to the tranquilized bear. As the helicopter's blades continued to rotate, a rush of wind enveloped the area, causing the bear's silvery fur to shine against the golden sunlight.

Expert hands and well-coordinated motorized straps ensured the safe transfer of the creature onto a specially designed stretcher. Jonathan's brow furrowed with concern as he surveyed the logistical challenge ahead.

"Moving a bear of this size requires precision and utmost care. We must be mindful of its weight and ensure it remains stable during transport."

Maria nodded in agreement; her eyes focused on the bear's colossal form. Together, they joined forces with the helicopter crew; each person assigned a specific role in the delicate operation. With coordinated efforts and meticulous attention to detail, they carefully loaded the bear.

The towering pines swayed forcefully as the aircraft lifted into the air. Meanwhile, inside the helicopter, the atmosphere was tense. The bear's vital signs steadily beeped on the monitor as every turn of the helicopter was executed with caution.

A ranger from the privately funded sanctuary, who was onboard the helicopter with them, leaned in to evaluate the grizzly.

"The bear's CO_2 is showing proper ventilation, and its heart rate is within a normal range. He appears to be responding well to the Ketamine."

When he spoke, the Chief's voice carried a note of relief.

"Transporting the bear to safety is good. Now, we must focus on ensuring its long-term survival. My people have had this plan in place for decades. We've known the bear, but the 'white man' did not, so we did not act until now. The Apache tribe in New Mexico will aid us. I believe its true sanctuary lies within the Sky Islands."

"The Sky Islands? I've heard of them, but I don't know much about them," said Maria. "What makes it an ideal refuge for the bear?"

Chief Grey Cloud's gaze held a depth of knowledge and wisdom.

"The Sky Islands are a place of exceptional biodiversity and natural beauty. We have long been communicating with members of other tribes who live there. They, too, know the spirit of the grizzly bear."

Maria's eyes lit up with fascination.

"It sounds like the perfect place. But how do we make it happen?"

The Chief's voice carried conviction. "We must collaborate with our counterparts, those who share our passion for conservation."

Chief Grey Cloud placed a hand on Jonathan's shoulder, his gaze filled with gratitude.

"Your dedication and expertise have brought us this far, Jonathan. Your partnership in this life is invaluable."

As the helicopter touched down, a sense of anticipation filled the air. Rumors had spread, whispers of the rare silver grizzly reaching the ears of those within the private sanctuary, and now they sought confirmation.

With gentle precision, the bear was carefully transferred from the helicopter to a secure holding area. Several tribal members at the sanctuary, with practiced expertise, minimized any disturbance to its tranquilized state while transferring.

Whispers of excitement rippled through the gathered crowd as they watched the massive form of the bear settle into its temporary enclosure. Eyes widened, hearts raced, and breaths held in anticipation, for this was a pivotal moment—a moment that could confirm the existence of the legendary Mexican grizzly bear.

The sanctuary staff worked swiftly yet meticulously; their movements were choreographed in harmony with the bear's dormant state. Under the watchful gaze of Jonathan, Maria, and Chief Grey Cloud, they performed a series of examinations and measurements to ascertain the bear's true identity. Maria meticulously examined its fur, scrutinized its size and proportions, and carefully observed its unique features—all with the hope of confirming the rumors that had circulated. As each examination and measurement unfolded, a collective sense of wonder and amazement permeated the atmosphere. The bear's distinctive traits hinted at the possibility of its true identity—an elusive grizzly believed by many to be lost to the annals of time.

"I'd heard stories of the Mexican grizzly bear from my grandparents, but I never thought I'd get to see one," whispered Kaya, a young wildlife enthusiast, her eyes wide with excitement. "Imagine the significance of this discovery!"

A spirited discussion ensued as the small numbered staff exchanged stories and knowledge about the historical presence of grizzlies in both Arizona and New Mexico. Whispers of legends and folklore, once thought to be mere myths, now carried a glimmer of truth.

Maria joined in the conversation, her eyes sparkling with excitement at what they had accomplished.

"This is a wake-up call. We must strive to protect not just this individual bear but also its habitat, ensuring that these magnificent creatures can thrive once again," added Jonathan to the group that had formed around them.

Amidst the exchange of ideas and shared passion, Chief Grey Cloud stepped forward, his voice commanding attention.

"Let us not forget the significance of this moment. The return of the Mexican grizzly bear carries a profound cultural significance for the indigenous peoples of this land. It is a testament to our enduring connection with nature and the need for its preservation."

Jonathan's gaze shifted. His voice was weighted with years of experience as he recognized the clamor of the surrounding crowd.

"We need to act fast. Once word gets out about this bear, it's gonna spread like wildfire. If you want my opinion, the world doesn't deserve to know."

VI: Sky Islands

JONATHAN, MARIA AND CHIEF GREY CLOUD retreated into a small hut on the outskirts of the sanctuary. They would have to commence the transport of the bear immediately if they wanted the operation to proceed safely and securely.

Jonathan and Maria quelled Chief Grey Cloud's concerns about the helicopter crew who had witnessed the bear.

"Ethan, our colleague, gave them very strict instructions about the classified nature of this mission," said Maria.

Jonathan couldn't help but notice how her eyes lit up when she said Ethan's name. He looked away and smiled quietly to himself.

Then he turned back and looked at the two of them. "We should get started immediately," he said. "So, how do we get to these Sky Islands?"

Chief Grey Cloud's lips unfurled into a knowing smile.

The landscape of the mountains stretched out underneath them in a truly mesmerizing sight. Maria, seated closest to the door, leaned her head slightly outside. She wanted to take the world in from up above – quickly –

before the pilot could ask her to return it. The air caressed her hair, and she closed her eyes. When she opened them, she got to experience the vision afresh. As the landscape widened before her in tandem with the chopper's ascent, she allowed herself to savor the moment.

The speakerphone in front of her seat rustled to life. The pilot issued a request for all passengers to refrain from the danger of leaning outside the aircraft.

Chief Grey Cloud was accompanied on the helicopter by three Apache men. Right now, the three men were engaged in a fervent discussion in their native language. Jonathan recognized it as either Lipan or Melascero Apache but wasn't quite sure. He had pulled a notebook out of his pocket and was jotting down the events of the past few days. He wanted everything to be on record for the book that he was writing – and he expected to be contacted by journalists soon, anyway. He didn't want to lose the essentials. As he was writing, Jonathan would occasionally glance up at the Apache men.

Chief Grey Cloud, who was peacefully detached from the ongoings of everything around him, paused and turned his head in the direction of his men.

"You're being impolite," he said in clear and enunciated English. "They know our people; we trust them."

The Apache men understood immediately and nodded their heads.

"Many apologizes," said one of them.

The three of them looked at Jonathan and Maria.

"We were just saying," said the one who'd spoken before, "that we've witnessed a spectacular miracle that could change the course of our people's history."

"If the world could learn from this," said another, "they would understand the significance of this event. The fact that we were able to find the bear is a message from nature. It is a wake-up call: it's telling us that nature is more powerful than man or animal."

"The recent increase," chimed in the third, "in efforts for the protection of the environment seem to have pleased nature. So, the world has been rewarded."

"The Dodo is a lesson in extinction. That was nature's punishment to us. But nature is just. Our efforts in these times have caused it to reward us now."

Jonathan had never thought of it like that, but he couldn't deny that there seemed to be a direct correlation.

"What a wonderful gift," Maria said softly. She was looking at the sleeping beast with a mixture of awe and affection.

"We are nature, and nature is within us," said one of the Apache men.

"But then again," said another, "We know this world and people are unkind to the planet, its animals and to each other. Because of this, maybe the people do not deserve to know of this gift."

"But then," said the first, "nature is sending the world a message; how do you get people to understand it?"

There was a reflective pause. Everyone mulled over the question in their own heads. The group was introspective for much of the remaining ride.

For an additional forty-five minutes, the journey continued, each passing moment adorned with breathtaking mountains, crystal lakes, and flowing streams. It was then that the Sky Islands revealed themselves. Stretching towards the heavens and rising high above the clouds, they stood as towering symbols of natural beauty, making it one of the most biodiverse places in the world.

By now, the bear was slowly awakening from its ketamine-induced slumber. It shifted slightly from its place in the helicopter, which was on a silky mat behind the area where the group was seated.

As Jonathan took in the view, his heart brimmed with joy, knowing that this place would become the bear's sanctuary. He found solace in the fact that it would be shielded from harm and remain hidden in this beautiful place. With caution, the helicopter gently descended, making contact with the ground.

While monitoring the bear's vital signs, Maria proceeded to release the straps that held the bear in place. Her gaze noted the rhythmic rise and fall of its chest with every breath. Carefully, she removed the EKG leads and pulse oximetry, ensuring the animal was stable.

"In this realm of ancient origins," the Chief spoke solemnly, "the spirits congregate, rendering this place truly sacred. Everything within it flourishes and prospers. It is the essence that draws us to bring the bear here, for our people yearn to see this creature thrive in all its splendor."

As if waiting for the Chief to finish his speech, the bear stirred and stretched. In a swift motion, it leaped out of the helicopter and swiftly sprinted into the swaying, towering grass.

Jonathan took a deep breath; a profound sense of relief washed over him. The mission was a success, and he felt an overwhelming sense of gratitude.

While Maria watched the bear sprint up the hill, a bittersweet realization overcame her - they would never lay eyes on this bear again. A lump formed in her throat, yet her heart felt full of air; at least it was safe.

When Jonathan turned to face her, he caught the solemn look in her eye. He felt exactly the same way.

With these emotions, a profound sense of pride enveloped him for being entrusted with such a mission. Not only had he contributed to saving a species, but he had also managed to penetrate the intangible barrier he had erected around himself after Marianne had passed away.

Chief Grey Cloud and his men were silent and meditative.

And then, as if to draw a curtain upon the mission that these people had embarked upon, darkness fell upon them.

Before the helicopter could safely transport the group back to Arizona, marking the culmination of their expedition, Chief Grey Cloud cleared his throat. The attention of all those on board shifted toward him.

"It's time that we must make a decision before we go back to our usual routines," he said in his usual solemn tone.

Maria and Jonathan exchanged puzzled looks.

"What decision, Chief?" inquired Maria, perplexed.

"Can we afford the world to know about that bear?"

With this question, a sense of realization hit everyone.

"But what would we say?" one of the Apache men chimed in.

Jonathan was deep in thought as he scratched his beard. "If we really want to protect the bear, we can't reveal its identity or location. I mean, look at all the challenges facing the Mexican grey wolf. In a world that is increasingly becoming divided, with one group supporting wildlife reintroduction and the other opposing it, the safety of the bear remains at risk."

"We must forge another story instead," he suggested.

"Absolutely. This news should not be revealed at any cost," the Chief said.

Meanwhile, Maria retrieved the hair follicles and blood

samples from her rucksack that she had collected from the bear and, in a fleeting motion, dumped all the contents out of the helicopter.

Everyone watched her with amused expressions.

"Now, the Mexican grizzly bear no longer exists! He only exists if we tell people," she smiled satisfactorily, removing every trace that might lead to the fact of the bear's existence.

"Perfect!" exclaimed Jonathan. "We will report that it was just a large black bear terrorizing the community. The same bear who killed Billy Herder's cow. So, we will convince the community that the bear has been relocated by White Mountain Apache Game & Fish, and there will be no more sightings of the bear or killing of the livestock. All agree?"

Impressed by the idea, everyone agreed instantly, and they all vowed never to mention a word about the Mexican grizzly bear to the outside world.

Contended by their consensual decision, Jonathan could not be happier, but as the helicopter touched down in a field adjacent to Mount Baldy, he felt a twinge of sorrow – this marked the end of their journey. The thought pierced his heart like a sharp dagger. He recognized all the joy he had discovered in the company of new friends and the reluctance to bid farewell. It had been a long time since he had embarked on such a journey – it felt good to be reconnected to the man he once was.

The moon cast its glow across the sky, which was littered with both stars and wisps of cloud. The group established their camp for the night, nestled on the banks of a small creek.

Jonathan lit a small campfire and began preparing dinner. It was a relief to him not to be concerned about the light that emitted from the flames. The grizzly was now in its new home and there was nothing to worry about.

Still, as they sat around the fire, talking, joking, and enjoying one another's company – for Jonathan, this was a first in a very long time – a large branch snapped. It came from behind them in the dark.

Suddenly, Dwayne Tompkins appeared once again. Illuminated by the golden glow of the flickering flames, he flashed his gap-toothed grin. His crew was positioned behind him.

"Well, looks like we meet again," he said, drawing out his words and enunciating every syllable.

Jonathan tightened his fist. His heart began to race.

"Tompkins," he seethed in a harsh whisper.

"Didn't mean to frighten ya'll," said Tompkins. He theatrically looked around and above him. "We heard a helicopter and thought we'd check it out."

Chief Grey Cloud calmly stared at the men. The Apache men looked at the Chief for direction. And Maria was focused solely on how angry Jonathan looked.

"Guess what, Crow? You're too late," said Tompkins, frowning sarcastically, "We got that bear. It belongs to us now!"

Jonathan didn't respond.

"Sorry to have beat ya to it. But it was my time to be famous, not yours."

"TOMPKINS!" Jonathan roared.

He hadn't realized that he'd stood up.

Chief Grey Cloud's men sprang up too. Maria was not sure how, but the three of them were suddenly armed; one held a pointed pistol while the others had pulled out rifles. They approached Tompkins threateningly.

"Leave!" exclaimed the one with the pistol, "You are not welcome here."

Tompkins delivered an exaggerated pout, his black eyes piercing the night.

"The bear is a spirit of the land; no mortal can capture it," said the Apache man.

"Is that so?" said Tompkins. He drew in a breath and was about to speak, but one of his crew mates tapped him on the shoulder. He whispered something into his ear, looking directly at the group.

Tompkins turned his head towards them again. "My apologies, friends," he said, "My man, Cash, here says we're running late. Keep an eye out for me in the papers."

He turned around as his crew began to leave but then looked back and said, in a mockingly high-pitched voice, "Toodle-oo!" wiggling his fingers.

Chief Grey Cloud only shook his head. He and his men, as before, did not join Jonathan and Maria in their respective tents that night.

To this day, it remains a mystery where the Apache men went to sleep. Perhaps it was that they loved nature so much that they would rather have slept in the great outdoors than confine themselves to synthetic tents.

In the morning, which was as glorious as their success, the group embarked on their journey toward the Apache camp. However, a growing unease settled within Jonathan as they pressed forward; an unsettling sensation gnawed at him. He didn't want this adventure to end and was reluctant to accept its conclusion.

So while the others talked, made little quips, and laughed, Jonathan remained awfully silent. He thought about Marianne and the fleeting nature of both experiences; his mind centered on how and why things must come to an end.

By midday, they had arrived at the Apache camp. Chief Grey Cloud organized a feast to celebrate the momentous occasion that had come to pass on the day before. For hours, the whole tribe celebrated. Jonathan and Maria were their guests and were treated with immense reverence and hospitality. By the time the sun began to grow dimmer, Jonathan realized that it was time to head home.

When he requested to take his leave, Chief Grey Cloud thanked him profusely.

"Every time we have needed you," said Chief Grey Cloud, "you have come to the aid of my people. We wish that all people were like you – lovers of nature, people, and the world."

Then he glanced at Maria. "This young girl," he said with a twinkle of pride in his eye, "has enormous potential."

Shortly, Jonathan and Maria packed their belongings and began hiking back towards Thompson Ranch. Their bellies were full of Indian fried bread as the birds twittered noisily about them.

They established a camp in the vicinity of an abandoned Boy Scout camp, nestled along the West Fork of the Black River. Jonathan wanted to revere in the beauty of the great outdoors – a realm that extended far beyond the walls of his cabin – but in a place that was still, very much, home.

The Mexican grizzly bear had left an indelible mark on him; the self-imposed isolation since the loss of Marianne was no way to live. It was his grief that caused him to withdraw, finding solace in the illusion of companionship through their memories together.

If Chief Grey Cloud hadn't called upon him for help, he would have never witnessed the miracle of seeing the last surviving Mexican grizzly.

The idea that this particular bear was the last of its species concerned Jonathan. He wanted its existence to endure. However, he found solace in the possibility that the bear might still engage in other reproductive endeavors. Throughout history, documented cases of ursid hybrids emerged, where the union between a grizzly and a brown bear resulted in offspring.

"What if there are no other Mexican grizzly bears," pondered Jonathan, his voice tinged with worry. "What are the chances that the species will survive?"

"Brown bears will mate with polar bears, black bears, and grizzlies," answered Maria. "But not a lot of research has been conducted on how well the gene pool will survive."

They sat by a fire that they'd built and sipped a cup of coffee. Jonathan looked around at the world around and above him. Stars spread out across the sky; it was as though a glittery canopy had been pulled overtop of them. But the sight was still incomparable to what Jonathan knew the grizzly would be experiencing in Sky Islands.

He gazed into the mountains ahead of him with his back towards the way home. He silently contemplated his journey and took another sip of coffee. Suddenly, Jonathan saw Chief Grey Cloud approaching from the distance on his horse.

"Chief!" Jonathan exclaimed. Maria stood up and laughed in surprise.

The Chief secured his horse to a tree and walked towards them, his silent and illuminating presence growing larger and more focused as he approached.

"My dear friends," he said, "I bring good news."

Jonathan stood up to greet him. Then, the Chief sat down with them by the fire.

"One of our scouts has checked on the bear to ensure its safety!" exclaimed the Chief. He pulled out a fabric drawstring bag and opened it.

Handing Jonathan a few rectangular pieces of paper with handwritten notes, the Chief watched as he accepted them with a mix of anticipation and caution. As Jonathan glanced at the topmost piece of paper, his face transformed into a delightful smile.

Chief Grey Cloud then handed him a set of photographs. It was a picture of the Mexican grizzly bear living in the Sky Islands... but it was not alone! The bear was surrounded by four others just like it.

Three of them, Jonathan noted, were female.

VII: Home Again

THE FIRE RUSTLED merrily in the corner. Jonathan felt glad to be home. It was quiet and peaceful here, but he wouldn't trade the adventure that he'd just had for anything.

As he settled into the chair in his living room, he picked up a framed photograph – A photo of Marianne and himself, the very same one that Chief Grey Cloud had admired during his last visit. His gaze lingered, transporting him back in time. Though it had only been five days since he departed on this adventure, his entire world had been transformed.

"Time is my new currency. I shall spend it well," he muttered to himself.

He put the picture on the coffee table and picked up his diary. He began to write:

Today has been a moment of profound realization for me. It has become clear that the essence of life is not about accomplishing more but rather becoming more. I find myself incredibly fortunate to have been part of a remarkable adventure that involved saving the life of a Mexican grizzly bear. I am left with both awe and concern.

I am struck by the relationship between technology and our connection with nature. In an age of constant connectivity, it appears people are increasingly becoming less connected to the natural world and each other. Life is not about creating highlight reels for others to marvel at. It's about creating deep connections with the world around us and allowing our experiences to emanate from that place! True fulfillment and meaning are not in superficial representations. Only forming genuine connections with nature and all living beings will satisfy the soul.

The sad reality is that if the world discovers the existence of these bears, their survival will be doomed.

One hour later, he made his way toward the village. Ethan and Maria had invited him for drinks at Molly Butler's, and the place was bustling with cabin renters.

"I hate this time of year," he grumbled quietly to himself, noticing that the lobby was filled with strangers, shoulder to shoulder, waiting for a table.

He looked into the bar and spotted the two of them sitting at a high top near the window. The evening sun cast a faint glow over their faces, and Jonathan smiled at the sight of them exchanging a private joke.

Ethan's attention was clearly on Maria.

"Presenting, Mr. Crow!" the bartender announced to the crowded bar, offering him a frosty pint of beer. "No need to get excited. I was warned you were coming in!" she quipped playfully.

"Much appreciated! Treating me like a true VIP, about time!" he responded with a chuckle, waving to Ethan and Maria. He walked over to their table, dragging an empty chair behind him, and sat down.

"So," he asked, "you know any of these people?"

"Not a single one!" Ethan said while shrugging his shoulders.

"We have a present for you," said Maria.

"Oh, really? What could that be?" asked Jonathan, frowning quizzically.

Ethan reached under the table and pulled up a brown paper bag. He placed it on the table and pushed it toward Jonathan.

"If you two got me a cellular phone," he said, "I'd like to clarify that I will never use it!"

They laughed and shook their heads.

"Just open it, please," said Maria, gesturing towards the package.

Jonathan looked at her tentatively and then at the package. He pulled it to his side of the table and reached inside.

He felt a cardboard box.

"Treasure," he commented, giving the couple a sidelong look.

However, as soon as he placed the box on the table and lifted the lid, his expression transformed. Inside, nestled carefully, lay a miniature wooden hand-carved grizzly bear.

"Thank you so much," said Jonathan.

"You're welcome," said the couple in tandem. Then they looked at each and broke into a laugh.

Jonathan finally relaxed, immersing himself into the busy atmosphere of the bar. He recalled his earlier thought about time being his new form of currency.

"It is up to me how I spend my time," he thought to himself.

With that thought, he abandoned the negative idea that the bar was just a busy place full of ignorant tourists. He began to savor each moment as he introduced himself to new people and engaged in meaningful discussion.

"Which Death Valley are you from?" asked one gentleman, referring to either Phoenix or Tucson.

"Neither. I live here in Greer," Jonathan replied with a sense of pride. "What about you?"

"Phoenix! It just hit 118 degrees today, but you know it's a dry heat!"

Jonathan laughed, "Phoenix, where the sun is always trying to kill you, but the Mexican food is totally worth it!"

Another patron, who had overheard the conversation, raised his glass of beer and said, "You actually live here? That is amazing! I'm from Tucson, where pool parties feel like hot tub confessions!"

"That constant feeling of having pancake batter in your boxer shorts isn't a pleasant one, that's for sure!" said Jonathan with a smile.

He finally made his way back to Ethan and Maria and said goodbye.

Eventually, after paying his bill, it was time to turn in and get some sleep. He was grateful to have enjoyed an evening out. As he drove home in his Land Cruiser, he felt like a much younger version of himself.

As he entered through the front door, he put on his slippers and walked inside. He remembered the book he'd gotten at the library and realized it was now overdue. He imagined the librarian out in the forest looking for him, trying to collect her twenty-five cents in overdue fees. It made him laugh as he turned off the lights and went to bed.

The following day, Jonathan tried to resume his regular routine. After enjoying breakfast and sipping his coffee, he embarked on his hike. Initially, he gravitated toward Marianne's beloved trail, but a surge of inspiration led him to venture off the beaten path. Amidst the trees, he spotted a sizable lobster mushroom emerging from the carpet of fallen pine needles - an edible delight he relished grilling. Without hesitation, he plucked it from the ground and carefully placed it into his rucksack.

Undeterred, he pressed onward, driven to conquer a peak he had not yet explored. Upon reaching the summit, a wave of accomplishment came over him. From that vantage point, he gazed at the distant Escudilla Mountain, reminding him of Aldo Leopold's essay, with its final sentence saying,

"Escudilla still hangs on the horizon, but when you see it, you no longer think of the bear. It's only a mountain now."

He was, of course, alluding to the grizzly bear that once roamed the Arizona White Mountains.

"Well, Mr. Leopold, if you're up there and looking down, it's time we rekindled our thoughts about that bear!" Jonathan whispered aloud.

By later that afternoon, Jonathan had made his way back to his cabin. As he gazed at the cabin's exterior, he felt the moment had come to begin the task of chinking and staining the logs. This was an activity he always appreciated. Transforming weathered wood was always a source of solace for Jonathan. The process felt almost meditative, offering him a way to connect with his purpose.

While he was in the process of sanding the south-facing wall, the sound of a vehicle approaching his driveway caught his attention. Wiping sweat from his brow, he walked around the cabin to see Chief Grey Cloud stepping out of his truck.

"Not again!" exclaimed Jonathan with a laugh.

"Jonathan, hello," the Chief responded, waving his hand.

After a quick embrace, Jonathan welcomed him inside. He walked into the kitchen, where he poured water into an electric kettle and made a cup of instant coffee for each of them.

He carried the cups into the living room, where the Chief was sitting down in Jonathan's favorite armchair.

Jonathan handed the Chief a cup of coffee and then plopped down on the sofa.

"Thank you," said the Chief as he began sipping his coffee.

"You're welcome," said Jonathan with a smile.

"I have some news for you," said the Chief.

Jonathan raised his brows. It seemed that everything was about surprises now.

"What could it possibly be?" he asked.

Chief Grey Cloud handed him a folded paper. It was The White Mountain Independent. Jonathan realized that he'd missed the morning news. He unfolded the paper and saw a headline, "Local Poacher Discovered Dead."

The article detailed the passing of Dwayne Tompkins. Apparently, last night, the Apache County Sherriff's Department had pulled his body from the Black River near Buffalo Crossing. His crew, who had been questioned, had been taken into custody.

Jonathan thought about the passing of this man. He briefly meditated upon his life. Chief Grey Cloud, seemingly in sync with Jonathan's thoughts, looked at him gravely and commented,

"Nature has taken the very man that fought it; he has met his end in the very place that he sought to destroy it."

He looked at Chief Grey Cloud solemnly. For sure, this was a horrible way to greet death. Greed takes people down a dark road, and unfortunately, it was a sad way to end a life.

Jonathan folded the piece of paper up again. He glanced at the picture of Marianne. Even in death, her spirit shone through the smile on her face. All of life comes to an end, and he really missed her.

VIII: Life Afterwards

SAVING AND RELOCATING the Mexican grizzly bear had left an imprint on Jonathan's heart, and soon he decided that he needed to continue with his efforts to help preserve the environment and its wildlife. He certainly had lost touch with this purpose when his wife passed away. In order to do so, he needed to engage with more people, converse, and spread awareness.

So, with a heart full of passion, Jonathan decided to start a new chapter of his life. He approached the educational system within the White Mountains, eager to contribute his expertise and spread knowledge. After much anticipation and a series of interviews, he finally received a letter that would allow him to start lecturing at Northland Pioneer College.

His first lecture was scheduled for Monday morning, a prospect that filled him with exhilaration. He embarked on his journey to the Show Low campus in his Land Cruiser, thoughts racing as he mentally rehearsed the information he was eager to impart to his students.

As he stood before the class, Jonathan began his lecture. He found himself entranced by the curiosity twinkling in their eyes, reminiscent of the same sparkle Maria had when their journey began. "If I inspire one Maria in this entire class, it will have been worth it,"

Jonathan muttered to himself. After a quick introduction, he emphasized his passion for the Arizona White Mountains and his desire to impart their beauty through education.

A student raised his hand and inquired, "Mr. Crow, have you ever come across a bear in the woods?"

There was some giggling amongst the other students.

Jonathan smirked and replied, "Oh if only you knew!"

His teaching had an irresistible allure, capturing their attention completely. Possessing the remarkable talent of great teachers, he could mentally transport his students beyond the classroom, enabling them to forge a connection with something larger than themselves.

As the day ended, Jonathan felt genuinely grateful for the chance to connect with young minds. During his drive back to Greer, he realized that students residing in the mountains already possessed an appreciation for their surroundings. His true mission was to connect with those 'cabin renters' and city dwellers who were new to the mountain experience.

Volunteering at the Butterfly Lodge Museum in Greer presented a perfect opportunity! The museum, housed in an original log cabin dating back to 1913, once hosted historical figures such as James Willard Schultz and Lone Wolf. Now transformed into a beautiful haven, it offered the perfect space for people to learn about the White Mountains and its captivating history. After all, creating meaning is what would ultimately foster a deep connection with the mountains.

With the passage of time, Jonathan's influence and his efforts to preserve wildlife grew far and wide. People from neighboring towns sought his wisdom, attended his lectures, and started engaging in thoughtful conversations about nature.

Amidst the whirlwind, Jonathan never let his book slip from his mind and eventually got it published. He donated several copies to the museum, committing a portion of the profits to support its cause. In his trusty Land Cruiser, he always kept a few copies to give to tourists exploring the area.

To make it easy for tourists to contribute, he cleverly positioned a mason jar discreetly behind the bar at Molly Butler's. The jar bore a simple 'Crow' label on its front. When people would offer to buy a book from him, he would suggest they go enjoy a meal at Molly's while casually slipping a dollar or two into the mason jar. This tactful strategy would then allow him to have drinks on the house without an ounce of guilt!

While he immersed himself in volunteer work and delivering lectures, Maria took another route. An exciting opportunity from the Arizona Game & Fish Department led her to serve there for a month. Filled with elation, she wasted no time in sharing the news with Jonathan, prompting him to invite her for breakfast at their customary spot, the Rendezvous Cafe. It had become a regular meeting place for them where they, along with Ethan, occasionally met to provide an update about their lives.

As she approached the table, Jonathan's gaze met hers, and a broad smile illuminated his face. He stood up to greet her, pulling her into an embrace that enveloped her with a sense of happiness. Although Jonathan and Marianne couldn't have children due to her endometriosis, Maria now filled a special place in his heart, offering him a connection he had never experienced before, almost like having a daughter of his own.

"Long time no see," he remarked, grinning warmly at Maria.

Returning the smile, Maria eased into her chair and sat at the table.

Just as their conversation was getting started, a familiar face emerged from behind the front door of the restaurant.

Maria's face lit up with delight as she spotted Ethan.

"Are the two of you dating?" Jonathan inquired with a slight smirk.

"Curiosity got the better of you?" Maria playfully inquired, sporting a mischievous smile as she stood and planted a kiss on Ethan's cheek.

Jonathan shook his head, unable to contain his amusement, and let out a hearty chuckle in response.

With a playful tone, Jonathan quipped, "Working together at Game & Fish now, huh? Isn't there a policy about dating co-workers?"

He turned to Ethan, teasing him about the demands of his job, saying, "I know your job can be tough!"

Then, he shifted his attention to Maria, genuinely curious, and asked, "And how about you, Maria? How is your job going?"

Maria's face lit up as she leaned forward, brimming with enthusiasm. She reached across the table, clasping Jonathan's hand, and delved into the details of her job with fervor. There was a sense of purpose in her voice as she recounted the thrilling projects she had been involved in and the profound impact they had made on wildlife conservation.

"Oh, Jonathan, it's been an incredible journey! I'm now their lead conservationist," she proudly declared, her sense of achievement evident with every word.

Jonathan marveled at the depth of her passion and the profound conviction that infused her words. He had always admired her dedication to wildlife and her relentless efforts to safeguard the natural world.

"That's truly amazing, Maria! Congratulations! Which assignment are you working on now?" he inquired eagerly.

With a new level of excitement, Maria leaned in closer. "I just completed a project on the Mexican grey wolf, and tomorrow I'll be giving a briefing about it. Would you like to join me?" she asked enthusiastically.

"Nah, I'm retired," he said jokingly. "Of course, I would. So, what's the new project?"

Ethan's face lit up with enthusiasm as he exclaimed, "Wait until you hear this!"

"Have you heard about Lil' Jefe?" she asked with a hint of mystery in her tone.

Jonathan furrowed his brow, trying to recall the name. "I remember El Jefe the jaguar?" he replied. "Lil' Jefe certainly doesn't ring a bell."

Maria's smile widened as she leaned back into her chair. "Lil' Jefe is Arizona's only known ocelot, and until yesterday, we were unsure whether it was still alive. But guess what? He's now been confirmed roaming the Huachuca Mountains, and we have visible evidence from a game camera!" she exclaimed, her eagerness palpable.

Jonathan's eyes widened with astonishment. "Wow! That's incredible!"

A sudden realization dawned on Maria as her eyes twinkled mischievously.

"But," she continued, "the assignment includes researching whether or not it has been separated from its family as a result of the border wall. I might need to hire some help. You wouldn't happen to know what a rucksack is, would you?"

They all burst into a fit of laughter.

***

"Ladies and gentlemen, thank you for gathering today to discuss the intriguing journey of Asha, the Mexican grey wolf. We are so pleased to announce that she has successfully returned to Arizona after straying from its designated recovery area. This was all made possible with the mutual efforts of the Arizona Game & Fish Department and the US Fish and Wildlife Service. According to the GPS coordinates, she had traveled more than 500 miles, crossing state lines and navigating a very challenging journey. This extraordinary event demands both our attention and admiration." Maria said as she keenly addressed the surrounding communities who had gathered to attend the meeting.

Maria, the passionate wildlife biologist, confidently addressed the audience from the front of the room, flanked by Ethan at a polished mahogany table. They were not alone, as other experts and officials had also gathered, all immersed in the captivating discussion about the two-year-old female wanderer wolf named Asha. Jonathan, with keen interest, stood in the corner of the room, chewing on a toothpick.

"Do we suspect any breeding while she was out of permitted territory?" one of the members asked.

This time Ethan responded, "We do not. Actually, it's been communicated already that prior controlled-breeding efforts were unsuccessful, which may explain its departure from the Rocky Prairie Pack. Further, she has been monitored with a radio collar since introduction."

As the meeting progressed and the discussion about Asha continued, one rancher asked with genuine curiosity, "Where was the wolf released?"

The room fell silent for a moment as all eyes turned towards Maria and Ethan, eagerly awaiting their response.

"Into the Apache-Sitgreaves National Forest," Maria replied. "I believe with every endangered species we relocate, save, and release, we are progressing to preserve our wildlife."

She smiled.

With a motion of her hand that held a small remote controller, she pressed the button as a large screen flickered to life, displaying images of Asha captured by trail cameras along her journey in the wild. The wolf's silvery-grey coat seemed to shimmer in the light.

With murmurs rippling across the room, someone complimented, "I must say, the photographs are amazing quality."

The attendees nodded, clearly impressed by the stunning visuals. Maria and Ethan both exchanged proud glances at one another, knowing their efforts had successfully conveyed the beauty of this particular wolf.

As Maria stood up from the table and approached the podium, she was eager to present further facts about the Mexican Grey Wolf Recovery program. However, before she could delve deeper, one of the ranchers politely said, "Miss Black?"

"Yes, sir. Go ahead," she said respectfully.

"Miss Black, I feel we've been provided with enough information about this Mexican grey wolf, but what can you tell us about the other Mexican species you were looking for? We would like to know more about the bear. We never got to hear any news about that," he said.

Maria cast a nervous glance at Jonathan, and so did Ethan.

While anticipating questions about their adventure, they hadn't expected them to be raised during this meeting. Their little adventure had not gone unnoticed, and they now realized that news of their expedition had spread rapidly. Although they couldn't identify the leaked source, they had known from the very beginning that their journey wouldn't stay concealed for long. In the back of their minds, they were positive that during their interrogation about Dwayne Tompkins' death, his crew had to have said something.

Prior to this meeting, a few ranchers and citizens had already approached Jonathan with the same question. In response, he started informing people from the surrounding communities that their encounter had been with a large black bear. His intention was to dispel any fears of a potential grizzly bear presence in the White Mountains. However, instead of receiving reassurance, Jonathan had encountered only pessimistic distrust from those he spoke to.

"Where's the proof?" the skeptics would ask whenever Jonathan recounted the tale of their adventure. So, eventually, he dropped the idea and declined to disclose any specific details. He was beginning to understand why people were distracted and disconnected from nature and the environment.

With this realization, he recalled that out of the fifteen hundred endangered species under the Endangered Species Act, comprising a third of the total, a hundred and fifty had tragically succumbed to extinction.

It was this sobering fact that further fueled his determination to persist. Jonathan decided that he needed to continue with his efforts to help preserve the environment and its wildlife without ever talking about his encounter with the grizzly bear.

However, he never imagined that questions about the bear would arise while on a live social media feed being broadcasted throughout the entire world! Nevertheless, they had already devised a plan and were going to stick to it.

With Jonathan's nod, Maria began, "It was all a misunderstanding. It was actually a large black bear that we found and relocated to a place where it can't harm further livestock."

Maria, Jonathan, and Ethan noticed that the audience was still dissatisfied. Some remained adamant, unconvinced by Maria's explanation, and continued to voice fears of potential livestock attacks. Even those who believed her seemed skeptical and demanded more details about their adventure into the wilderness.

Sensing the tension and the possibility of another question about the Mexican grizzly bear, Maria swiftly redirected the conversation, saying, "Let's stay on topic and focus on the Mexican grey wolf. The story of Asha is a remarkable—"

"But where exactly did you find this black bear?" one local citizen interrupted, curiosity clearly etched on his face.

"Near the Black River on the White Mountain Apache Indian Reservation," Maria replied nonchalantly. She did not want to go into the details.

"But why are there no pictures of that bear? You have got all these pretty photos of the wolf. My guess is that Game & Fish is hiding something. What is it that you aren't telling us?" one of the members of the audience chimed in.

After a moment of nervousness, Maria quickly gained her composure and responded, "Given that the animal was wild, our primary concern was ensuring the bear's safety and the safety of our team. Hitting the target with a tranquilizer requires a significant team effort, and our focus was to relocate the bear to a secure environment rather than take photographs."

"Ladies and gentlemen," Jonathan spoke finally.

He instantly became the focus of attention. He had been quiet throughout the meeting, but now it was his turn to speak.

"I understand your concerns about a reported grizzly bear in our region. We have thoroughly investigated the matter and can confirm that it was indeed a large black bear that was spotted in the area. It was discovered living on the Apache Indian Reservation, and due to its location on tribal land, we had to proceed with utmost respect for the tribe's sovereignty. Therefore, in coordination with the White Mountain Apache Game & Fish, it was decided to relocate the bear out of the state."

He paused briefly, then continued, "Since these black bears are not endangered species, taking their pictures was pointless. It was important to safely remove the bear from this territory so that livestock would remain safe."

A few of the faces seemed satisfied now.

Jonathan noticed Maria's unsteady hands clutching the edges of the podium, revealing the internal struggle she had faced while upholding the department's decision to withhold the true identity of the bear.

The room fell into a tense silence as the audience absorbed this information. Jonathan could sense their disappointment, suspecting that some of them saw through his carefully crafted response.

As the tension gradually eased, the audience reluctantly accepted the explanation. They may not have been entirely convinced, but Jonathan's comment seemed to bring a semblance of closure to the matter.

As the meeting ended, Maria and Ethan came to Jonathan.

With worried eyes, Maria voiced her concern, "I don't know how long we can keep this up."

"As long as they don't discover those hair samples you tossed out of the helicopter, I reckon we'll be ok," Jonathan replied, winking reassuringly at her.

IX: Conclusion

EIGHTEEN MONTHS LATER, Jonathan found himself gathering supplies at Western Drug in Springerville. While inspecting the displayed guns within the glass case, his attention was drawn to a television behind the counter, broadcasting the news. The sight of workers and shoppers gathering around it piqued his curiosity.

As he approached the television, he witnessed footage of a sizable group of grizzly bears in a wilderness area unfamiliar to him. Then, the news anchor started to report about the return of the Mexican grizzly bear to the Apache-Sitgreaves National Forest.

They had found their way back home.

"This particular bear species," stated the newscaster, "previously considered extinct under the Endangered Species Act, may soon be delisted if it establishes a sustainable population."

Observing the reactions of the employees and customers around him, Jonathan noticed a mix of elation and concern over the discovery.

The news anchor continued, "Despite potential delisting, the species will remain protected under the Endangered Species Act of 1973. The Arizona Game & Fish Department, in collaboration with the White Mountain

Apache Tribe, has temporarily closed the forest until further notice."

"Wow. Grizzly bears in Arizona!" The news anchor improvised, clearly not using his teleprompter.

The phone rang from behind the counter. An employee answered it, his gaze still fixed on the television screen.

"Western Drug. Can I help you? Yeah, he's here," he said, glancing over at Jonathan.

"Crow, you still don't have a cell phone?" he teased him. "It's for you!"

Jonathan navigated through the crowd of chattering customers, still discussing the grizzly bear news coverage.

"Hello," he greeted, keeping an eye on those around him.

On the other end of the line was Maria.

"Did you see the news?" she asked.

"Yeah. I'm at Western Drug... but I guess you knew that already," he replied.

"Jonathan, this is incredible! It hasn't been made public yet, but there are about six or seven Mexican grizzly bears that have returned to the area!" Maria exclaimed with excitement.

"Can you meet me and Ethan at Three Forks tomorrow? Does 7 a.m. work?" Maria asked.

"Yes, of course!" responded Jonathan as he handed the phone back to the store employee.

Suddenly, a familiar face in the crowd approached Jonathan; it was Billy Herder.

"I told you so," he said to Jonathan in a joking manner.

"Oh, I had no doubt you saw what you saw, Billy!" He admitted. "The thing is, people weren't ready to know the truth," Jonathan said. "How is your health doing?"

"Oh, one day, they say I'm gonna die, and the next day I wake up, still alive. Who knows? Hell doesn't want me and heaven is still undecided," Billy said with a smile.

"Well, you take care of yourself!" said Jonathan, making his way to the cashier to checkout. As he walked out of the store, he was immediately surrounded by several reporters and cameras asking questions about the grizzly bears in the White Mountains. What amazed Jonathan most was that these weren't just local reporters; they were from Phoenix.

Refusing to answer any questions, he made his way to his Land Cruiser, where he was successfully able to drive away.

He was reminded of how viral the world had become. The news was out, and that wasn't good for the bears.

The following day, Jonathan woke up, quickly brewed a cup of black coffee, and fried a single egg. He hopped into his Land Cruiser and set off toward Three Forks while constantly checking his rearview mirror to ensure he wasn't being followed.

Though Maria hadn't revealed the reason for their meeting, he had an inkling deep inside.

As he drove down Highway 273, Jonathan noticed several vehicles being directed to turn around by Highway Patrol, who had set up a blockade with blinking yellow lights just beyond the Big Lake turn-off.

"Good morning, Pete!" Jonathan called out.

"Mr. Crow, good to see you. Quite the story, isn't it?" the officer replied. "One moment, and we'll let you through."

He then signaled a few other patrol members to open up the barricade, allowing Jonathan to pass.

"Quite the story, indeed," Jonathan mumbled to himself as he drove through.

Ethan, and Chief Grey Cloud standing next to their vehicles in the turn-off.

"Jonathan, we meet again!" said Chief Grey Cloud, embracing him warmly.

"Let me guess. You didn't bring me out here to go fly fishing?" Jonathan quipped.

"No. I didn't," the Chief said, grinning mischievously.

"Let's go!" urged Maria as she started hiking down into the breathtaking Three Forks Valley.

The East Fork of the Black River was at its highest level in years due to the ample snowpack from the previous winter.

As they rounded a bend, their eyes widened in awe at the sight that unfolded before them. Six majestic Mexican grizzly bears were grazing peacefully in the sunlit meadow. One among them had skillfully snatched a brown trout from the stream and begun savoring its meal.

They all stood in reverent silence, soaking in what clearly was a miracle.

Maria couldn't contain her excitement and whispered, "Jonathan, can you believe it? It's beyond amazing!"

Jonathan's eyes shimmered with wonder as he replied, "There are no words. This is truly a once-in-a-lifetime experience."

Gazing at the magnificent creatures, they all felt humbled by their resilience. Their hearts brimmed with gratitude for witnessing the revival of such a glorious species, and they knew this encounter would forever be etched in their souls.

Finally, with a resonating voice, Chief Grey Cloud spoke, "The trail of the grizzly has not been forgotten."

The End.

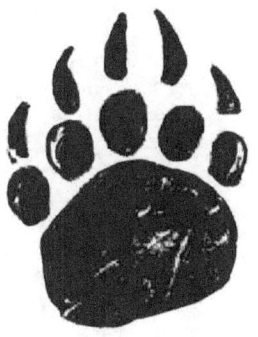

www.ingramcontent.com/pod-product-compliance
Lightning Source LLC
Chambersburg PA
CBHW060649260626
47161CB00008B/3069